The Onlyhouse

Teresa Toten

NORTHERN LIGHTS YOUNG NOVELS

Red Deer College Press

Northern Lights Young Novels are published by
Red Deer College Press
56 Avenue & 32 Street Box 5005
Red Deer Alberta Canada T4N 5H5

Acknowledgments
Edited for the Press by Tim Wynne-Jones
Cover art by Jeff Hitch
Text design by Dennis Johnson
Printed and bound in Canada for Red Deer College Press

Financial support provided by the Alberta Foundation for the Arts, a beneficiary of the Lottery Fund of the Government of Alberta, and by the Canada Council, the Department of Canadian Heritage, and Red Deer College.

COMMITTED TO THE DEVELOPMENT OF CULTURE AND THE ARTS

Canadian Cataloguing in Publication Data

Toten, Teresa, 1955–
The onlyhouse

(Northern lights young novels)
ISBN 0-88995-137-3

I. Title. II. Series.
PS8589.O83O64 1995   jC813'.54   C95-910457-7
PZ7.T67On 1995

Author's Acknowledgments

Thank you. Thank you. A tub full of thank yous could not begin to express the gratitude I feel for Peter Carver, who was there at the beginning, middle and end; Margaret Morin and Loris Lesynski, who typed hundreds of thousands of drafts almost without complaint; the brilliant group of writers struggling with me in the basement of Mabel's Fables; Tim Wynne-Jones, who tried very hard to beat this into the best book it could be; my dear abused friends, who were forced to listen to incoherent chapters over and over and over again; Sasha and Nikki, who make me strong; and, finally, my husband, Ken, who said, *"This* is going to be your year."

Za moju mamu, uvjek
(For my Mama, always)

My father died of pneumonia. That's *pne*umonia. For years I thought he died of *ammonia* until my grade three teacher explained that ammonia was a cleaning solvent. So unless he drank the ammonia, which would have been stupid, he must have died of pneumonia.

Anyway, because he's dead, Mama and I just have each other and we're poor. At least, we used to be.

Poor people live in flats and apartments. Rich people live in houses. See, we've been saving and saving my whole life. This summer we bought a house. We bought an Onlyhouse: a single, detached family home that costs a whole lot more than the stuck together kind. It's on Cleveland Street; that's along Davisville between Bayview Avenue and Mount Pleasant. I love to say the area over and over again. It sounds so elegant.

My Onlyhouse has reddish-brown bricks, and there's a small green porch in the front. All the front porches here are really little. Rich people don't sit on their porches. People sit in their backyards because they've got them. That's why it's so quiet. We also have a great big oak door. All of our neighbors' doors are painted in different colors. The real estate man said that the wooden door made our house "distinctive."

7

That's a nice way of saying "different." As soon as we get some money, I'm going to get Mama to paint it.

The whole neighborhood is full of big Onlyhouses. They don't let you grow vegetables in your front yard here. Instead, everybody has a maple tree and regular grass. As far as I can figure out, we're the only Catholics. Everybody else is Canadian. In the fall, I'm going to a school with no nuns in it. I think we're also the only ones without a car. We don't need one, of course, because neither Mama nor I know how to drive. We're going to rent the garage. I've already written up the notices in magic marker: Charming Garage For Rent. Only $15 A Month! Please Call —. Then I did our phone number in little strips underneath, so people can just tear it off. It's not rented yet.

Even though our Charming Garage sign is hanging on their bulletin board, Mama and I don't do any of our shopping at the Bayview Loblaws. I think it costs too much, but Mama says that Canadians don't know anything about food. Mama likes to feel her food, and everything in the Bayview Loblaws is wrapped in plastic. So we go to the Jewish market. We go every single Saturday morning. I love going to the Jewish market. It's near where we used to live. The best part about going is coming back.

To get there we take a bus, the subway and a streetcar. Buses are for rich places. I'd never been on one till we moved here. Buses drive by Onlyhouses, fabric stores and antique shops. They don't drive by gift stores with colored glass things in the window. You know, like the pink and orange Jesus, the one with the heart in the middle of his chest all stuck with thorns. Canadians buy their Jesuses on the main floor of the downtown Eaton's.

The bus drives right into the Davisville Subway

Station. It's a rich subway station. The men all have
suits and briefcases, and the women all wear lipstick,
except for Mama. You've got to be careful about waiting for the subway. There's a yellow and black check-
ered line near the edge of the platform. If you step
over the line, the subway will whoosh by and slice your
legs off. If you live, they put you in those commercials
where you have to sell key chains and tell other kids
about what a stupid thing you did. We ride on the
subway for eleven stops. Then we get to the streetcars.

Streetcars are for poor places. I can tell right away
now. The signs aren't in English, or if they are, they're
weird. We used to live on top of a store—Hakim's
Fine Furniture and Children's Clothing. It sold snow-
suits and kitchen tables at *"Low, Low Prices!"* Another
thing is that the blouses never match the skirts in the
dress shop windows. Everything matches on Bayview.

I used to think you had to be careful about streetcars, too. It's their faces. Some streetcars have big
round windows with raised eyebrows, which make
them look like they're surprised to see you. They're
the best. Other streetcars have square windows and
they look bored. They're okay. Then there's the kind
where the windows cross straight down to the car's
nose. They're creepy. When I was a kid, no matter
what Mama said or did, I never got on creepy streetcars. I do now of course because I'm almost eleven.

Even if you close your eyes you know you're in the
market. For one thing, except for prices, nobody can
speak English. Everybody can say, "Forty-seven cents a
pound," but that's about it. It's also the smells. I guess
I miss the smells. There aren't any on Cleveland
Street. The Jewish market smells like a kitchen. There's
fish and cheese and fruits but, best of all, there's the
smell of steaming hot bread just coming out of the

oven. Mama buys me the kind you have to tear off in chunks. Once you've eaten it, it lies around in a corner of your stomach for the rest of the day.

Right beside the bakery is the place that sells beautiful real live chickens. Mama says Chinese people buy them for pets, and I always pretend to believe her. We say hello to the Jamaican lady who owns the Chinese chickens. She sort of speaks English and everything, but, after the "Hello, how are you?" part, none of us really understands the other, so we just nod and smile a lot.

We go to Mr. Goldman, the kosher butcher, to buy our minced beef. You can tell a kosher place because it has a big yellow star in the window. There are a lot of yellow stars in the market. If there's a line-up, I try to break my sawdust pile record. They throw sawdust all over the place to catch the bloody drippings from the meat. Otherwise, all your best customers would be slipping around in pools of beef blood. Last week I finished seven mounds before Mama even got served. After Mr. Goldman's, we have to go to the Ukrainian butcher for pork hocks and salami. Kosher people don't eat pigs because it made them all get sick after Jesus died.

Next we go to the cheese store, where Mama and Mrs. Kostakis scream at each other about the price of strudel cheese. I never used to mind about the yelling before. I know they like each other. It's just that Mrs. Kostakis's English is just awful and Mama's is worse. What if someone from Cleveland Street walked in? When it's time to pay, Mama always insists she's never coming back and Mrs. Kostakis always insists she wouldn't let her. Finally, we lug our bags back onto the streetcar, the subway and the bus—back to our new home—back to our Onlyhouse.

10

We've got lots of room for the groceries. There's hardly any furniture and the rooms are so big. Mama sleeps on the pullout couch in the living room, and I have my very own brand new single bed in the dining room.

We've already rented out the second floor for $95 a month. A German lady from England lives there, but she's never home. She works all day and goes to school most nights. Mama thinks she's great because she's clean and she doesn't have a boyfriend. Mama says all Germans are clean and don't have boyfriends. I think the lady's great because she's pretty well invisible. It's easy to pretend we have the whole house to ourselves.

There's nobody around, so I don't have any best friends yet. I used to have a best friend—two really, Moshe Shenkman and Shernee Chandaria. Moshe's a Jew and Shernee's an Indian. Not an Indian Indian; an Indian from India; the ones with the dots on their foreheads. There aren't any kind of Indians in this neighborhood. "Just Canadians," the real estate man said. I bet they really miss me.

Mama says the kids here all go away to cottages for the summer. I just know they're going to like me. What's not to like? I look real Canadian and I live in an Onlyhouse. Whenever anybody asks where we're from, Mama makes me say "Croatia." Then, only if they've never heard of it, I'm supposed to say, "I was born in the city of Zagreb." I hate that. Nobody's ever heard of either place. Anyway, they've got to come back next week, the kids I mean. Grade six starts next week. I'm going to have a million friends next week. God, I can't wait until next week.

I knew the braids were a mistake.

Absolutely nobody wears braids. I told Mama. I said, "Mama, a ponytail, yes, a hair band even better, but these kids will *not* be wearing braids."

Would she listen? Immigrants wear braids.

You see, Mama's got to do my hair the night before. Braids stay tidy and don't hurt. Ever try sleeping in a ponytail? Mama has to be at work by 6:30 a.m. It's three buses and two subway stops away, which means she has to leave by 5:00 a.m. Mama works in the cafeteria of the Central Mortgage and Housing Corporation. She has to make sure all the vice presidents get their toasted Danish. I just say she works for the federal government. Every single morning Mama leaves me a pancake to warm, and every single night she braids my hair.

If I had a hair band, I could do it myself. They're three for a dollar at Honest Ed's, in the most fabulous colors. Mama says that hair bands are for lazy cigarette-smoking people. I think she means Canadian moms, but she never comes right out and says so.

Anyway, there I was, Room 501, Maurice Cody Public School. I'm the last one, in the last row. They do things alphabetically here. The teacher is standing in front of the blackboard, except that the blackboards are green. I bet green blackboards cost more than black blackboards. Everything looks expensive.

"Listen up, boys and girls," she tinkled. Her voice actually tinkled. Nuns don't tinkle.

"My name is Mrs. Glad. Welcome to the 1968–69 grade six class, your final year of junior public school." Then she stopped and blinked at everybody like she was waiting for something. "Yes, well, before we have roll call, I would like to introduce a lovely new addition to our little school."

Oh God.

"Lucy . . . come up here to the front, dear. Boys and girls, I would like you to meet Lucy Reza Voo, Vuh, Va— oh my!" There's snickering.

"How *do* you pronounce your last name, dear?"

"Uh, Vakovik," I blurted. It's really more like *Vook*oveech, but I thought Vakovik would sound more . . . I mean less . . . well, it didn't. Some of the kids were snorting.

"Lucy comes to us from St. Therese of the Flowers," Mrs. Glad whispered. Twenty-seven sets of blue eyes strained to hear her. "And there, she was at the top of her class in grade one, grade two, grade three, grade four and grade five. Isn't that splendid?"

I was ruined. I stood there with a face-hurting grin, sweat trickling down my back and drizzling into my underwear. Why was she doing this to me? What had I ever done to her? Lucy Vakovik, brown eyes, braids *and* a browner.

I spent recess in the third stall of the girls' washroom.

The rest of the morning limped along. Mrs. Glad outlined the work program. As far as I could tell, grade six was going to be a repeat of the stuff we did in grade four at St. Therese's. When the lunch bell rang, I hit the street so fast I forgot which way was home.

"Yoo-hoo, Lucy. *Lucy* wait up." I turned. Emily McDonald came flapping toward me. Emily McDonald's house is right behind mine; our backyards touch. They must be one of those cottage families because I hadn't seen them until this weekend. Emily has seven rose bushes, a lilac tree and a yellow swing set with an attached slide. What did they need a cottage for?

"Hi," she said to my feet. "I missed you at recess."

"Yeah, well, see . . ." I said.

"I thought, I've been thinking that since we're neighbors and everything, we could walk to school and back together, all the time, sort of."

"That'd be neat," I said.

"Super! And maybe you'd like to join Girl Guides with me perhaps, my mother could drive us to all the meetings since we've noticed you don't have a car, they're on Thursday nights at seven-thirty, you learn to sew, make campfires and strive for new badges, of course, they say, or at least Mother does, that Guiding expands your horizons and fosters community spirit." She finally exhaled.

I don't know. This Girl Guide stuff sounded like a lot of work. I reexamined her. See, Emily McDonald was wearing this stiff green and yellow dress with party shoes and hair ribbons that exactly matched her socks. She looked like it was picture day. We had this type at St. Therese's, but they were usually Estonian. They always latch onto the new kid because they don't have any friends left over from the year before. She did have a neat smile, though. There was something different about it.

"I'll have to ask Mama—uh, my mother," I said.

"Of course, sure, yes," she nodded.

14

We got to my house. "See you after lunch," she called. "Oh, I should warn you, stay away from Jackie Lewis, third row, second from the front. She's very disgusting and she always gets people to do exactly what she wants. I'll come by for you at precisely twelve forty-five. Bye-bye for now."

Hmmm.

I let myself in and turned on *The Edge of Night* on the TV. Then I warmed up some cabbage rolls.

Emily's mother was probably making her Kraft Macaroni and Cheese. They have it at the Bayview Loblaws, but Mama says it's one of those lazy people things. They make the most brilliant commercials.

I was on my second cabbage roll when I decided it was a do-or-die day. By 9:15 a.m. I'd been tagged as a goody-goody immigrant browner with braids. This was not good. This needed fixing. This needed a plan. Unfortunately, I didn't have one.

Emily and I chattered all the way back after lunch. Actually, Emily did most of the chattering, but that was okay since she knows absolutely everything about everybody. All the kids have a mom and a dad, except for Jackie Lewis. Her parents are divorced, or at least they would be, if Mrs. Lewis could find Mr. Lewis to divorce him. He took off four years ago. Mrs. Lewis is cocktail hostess at the Silver Rail Tavern on Bloor Street. Neither of us really knew what that was, but it sounded spectacular. "My mother works for the federal government." I paused and looked around. "Top-Secret, For-Your-Eyes-Only type of stuff."

"Wow!" her eyes light up. "That's so–o–o–o neat and exciting and fabulous!"

I liked Emily. The smile . . . I figured out her smile. Emily had a disappearing dimple. Just one, and

sometimes it was there when she smiled and sometimes it wasn't. I wondered if she knew.

I strolled into Room 501 like I owned the place. It
was perfect. Then Jackie Lewis charged right into me.
"Hey, ya little browner," she sneered, "what kind of
DP name is *Vack-a-shmick?*"

"Vakovik!" I said. "It's Croatian." Nothing. "I was
born in Zagreb." I tried for a defiant toss of my head,
but my stupid braids just whipped around and hit me
in the face.

"Ha!" she sprayed. "Never heard of it! Well, wop,
I've got a fist with your name on it. See you at recess."

What did I do? What, what, what? Was this some
sort of Protestant thing? Emily McDonald was looking
at me mournfully from the middle seat in the middle
row. "And, no hiding out in the girls' can, you little
suck!"

I prayed for an act of God, nothing major, just a
little something. He was busy. The recess bell rang at
2:15 p.m. "Okay, there's no need to panic," I mumbled on the way out. "Jackie's taller, but I'm fatter—
not fat—just fatter. Jackie's the oldest in the class. I'm
the youngest. Jackie has definitely fought before and I
. . . well, I'm fatter. Oh God."

"Over here, wop!" a voice called out of nowhere.
A very tidy ring of grade sixes had formed in the middle of the baseball diamond. Someone shoved me in.
Jackie was in the middle. I tried to say something
funny, but I was hyperventilating.

"Earrgh!" I squeaked.

"Get her, Jackie," someone called.

"Oh yeah!" she snarled and she grabbed my
braids. So . . . I kicked her in the stomach. It wasn't
like on TV. We mainly rolled around and around not
doing much of anything. Every so often I'd push her

face in the dirt, and then every so often she'd push my face in the dirt. This went on for about forty-seven hours. Finally, God remembered me and sent Mrs. Glad.

"No, no, no, *no*. People!" She was galloping toward us.

"I'll do the talking, wop," spat Jackie.

"We'll get the strap!" I shuddered. "I hate the strap. I can't stand the strap. God, strapped on the first day of school!"

"They don't strap here, stupid." She examined me. "You been strapped?"

"What's this? *What is this?*" interrupted Mrs. Glad. She had come to a full stop, but her body was still waving and heaving. Everybody else disappeared.

"It was a grave misunderstanding, Mrs. Glad," said Jackie. "I thought that Lucy here had said something derogatory about my family situation." And *she* called *me* a browner? "But, then I realized that she's new and she wouldn't even know about my dad and all. We were just clarifying the situation when you arrived."

"Is this how it happened, Lucy, dear?" she asked, not taking her eyes off Jackie.

"Yes, ma'am," I gulped. "It's all very clarified now."

"I see," she nodded. "Okay, a mistake is a mistake. Shake hands, girls, and walk back to class together."

On the way back Jackie hissed, "The strap, eh, wop?"

"Yeah, sure—all the time!" I said. "My hands are just healing over from last June." Actually, I'd only been strapped once, and then Sister Magdalene cried more than I did. "Yup," I heard myself say, "there's nothing like a nun for all-out brutality. The straps are three feet long, and every single nun carries one, always. They hide them in those black robes, underneath a big gold crucifix. Think about that for a while."

"*Jeez . . .*" she said. "You're okay, wop."

Now, Jackie did not beat me up. I'd say it was a tie. In fact, if anything, I'd say I did more of the beating, but a tie will do. We were alone in the stairwell. I turned and looked her straight in the face. "My name is Lucy. Call me Lucy." Jackie glared at me, then roared. I think she was laughing, but I wasn't sure. The stair rails shook. When she stopped, she stood there shaking her head.

"Let's get something straight," she said. "You're new and you haven't got it figured out yet. I own this place. Ask anybody. Maurice Cody is mine and before me, five years ago, my big sister Carole owned it. What I say goes around here. Mine. Got it?"

I knew the next few seconds were important, serious, big stuff. I was scared. "I got it," I said, "but my name is still Lucy."

She stared at the floor and spit. Then she turned her head just a little and caught me with the corner of her eye. "Okay, okay." She grinned and swung her arm around me. "You got it, *Lucy.* Amigos, okay?"

I don't remember if I smiled. I don't remember nodding. I do remember staring at the bubbling glob of spit on the school floor.

Chapter Two

I'd been in Room 501 for two weeks when Mama said she was "prouded" of me. She said it in English. I keep reminding her about the extra "ed" she sticks on things. She keeps forgetting. I used to spend hours teaching her in our old kitchen on top of Hakim's. We never got past my grade three phonics workbook. Mama said her head was too crowded to make room for the English words. That's why we always talk in Croatian. It's great in a way. We can say anything about anybody, and nobody understands but us.

I had just come from supper at Emily McDonald's house. I was sitting on my bed in the dining room explaining about how popular I was while Mama put away my freshly ironed clothes.

"It's not just Emily, Mama. The whole class treats me like I'm a regular person. Why, even Jackie's best friends, Jenny Clarke and Cindy Spencer, share their recess snacks with me."

Mama nodded and transformed all of my socks into perfect balls.

"But . . . the most amazing incredible thing is that Jackie Lewis invited me to dinner for Thursday night!"

That's when she said she was "prouded" of me. "That's nice, Lucija." She opened my underwear draw-

19

er. "But, of course, we first have to ask Emily for dinner. Then . . ."

Uh-oh.

"Then we'll ask Jackie's mother for permission, but not on a Monday or Wednesday." See, Mama cleans Taylor, Laidlaw and Abromovitz on Mondays and Wednesdays. They're a bunch of lawyers. She cleans them from 7:00 to 10:00 p.m. She cleans on Saturday mornings, too, but then I go with her and help.

"Um . . . y'know, Mama . . ." I got up to help her. "It's different here. These people—well, you don't have to have them over in strict order. It's more last minute, like today at Emily's. Why, we probably aren't expected to have either of them back this year even."

"I could make something Canadian," she said. "What do they eat for dinner? I know—roasted beef, they eat roasted beef all the time with a pudding."

Oh God.

"What did you have at Emily's?"

"Well, we had pork chops, mashed potatoes and a salad with Green Goddess dressing. Great name, awful taste."

"I could do pork chops," Mama said to my blouses.

"Yeah, well, then we played in their library. Can you believe that, their own library! It's a whole room full of books that they get to keep on their own walls. Oh, we're writing a mystery book. It's mainly my idea, but she's real good at turning ideas into regular words. She says that so far it's better than any of the books on her walls."

"Such a nice girl. Is the mother nice?"

"Yeah, sure Emily's okay. She has a disappearing dimple."

"A what?"

"Yeah. Sometimes it's there as plain as day when

she smiles, sometimes not. I'm trying to figure it out. It makes her look sort of mysterious."

"Tell her."

"No way!"

Mama shrugged. "What is Mrs. McDonald like?"

"She's okay, too. She said I was 'delightful,' and I'm welcome back anytime."

"That's it." Mama shut the drawers. "Such a nice lady. I'm going to call her right now to invite Emily for dinner." Mama marched over to the telephone. "Here—you talk!" She shoved the receiver at me. Mama doesn't ever really talk on the phone if she can help it, unless it's her Croatian friends. Her English completely disintegrates on the telephone, and she just ends up saying, "Ya, good, ya" all the time. I've had to cancel three subscriptions to the *Toronto Star* so far.

I put the phone down. "Mama! You've never even met her! And it's not—we don't, uh, oh jeez, look at the time. You're late for Taylor, Laidlaw and every-body!" I grabbed her coat and gave her a kiss. I'd have to think of something. I was kind of hoping to keep Mama under wraps for a while. Not forever, just a year or so until I got myself, you know, going.

After Mama left I did our monthly accounts. Mr. Abromovitz showed me how when we bought the house. Every month I go through the bills and bank statements and I get the mortgage, hydro, heating and telephone checks ready for Mama's signature. I also write polite letters to people who ask for money, like the Lung Association and the United Way. I have to explain about how we don't have any extra. That's except for the Salvation Army. We give them five dol-lars a year no matter what. Mama likes the uniforms.

I was rifling through our Birk's Box of Extremely Important Papers, thinking about going to Jackie's when I found it. It was an old scrap of paper stuck in a corner of the lid. I was going to throw it away, but then I noticed the writing. Mama's wobbly writing. It said, "Adam died today. Tuesday, April 16, 1957." That's all.

Adam was my father. Why did she write it down? I knew I was little when he died, but the date meant I was only six months old. God. I used to tell myself I could remember these big gentle hands. . . . I guess not. Can you remember something about someone you don't remember?

Boy, they weren't even married for two years. That's why Mama doesn't talk about him! She couldn't have known him very well. She tells me about how they took him away to the hospital, but that story always makes her crazy. See, the ambulance had the siren on and everything. Everyone knew he was dying. He knew. He kept apologizing. Right before it happened, he told Mama to bring me in so he could see me one more time. Well, I guess there are rules about babies in hospitals. They wouldn't let her. Mama begged and cried and yelled, but they still said no. So he died and he didn't ever get to say good-bye.

Maybe they just didn't understand her.

Chapter Three

*M*ama wanted me to bring flowers. I refused. "Cultured people don't go to a dinner without a gift for the hostess," she said, talking in Croatian as usual.

Oh God.

"I didn't bring flowers to Emily's!"

"That was different," she said. "It was last minute. You don't get flowers for last minute."

"Canadians don't get flowers period! I mean, not the kids. Mama, the rules are different here."

"Fine," she smiled, "you give them to Mrs. Lewis. Tell her they're from our garden."

"Look, I'll give her a pack of matches." Yeah, I bet Jackie would like that. Mama has a collection of matchboxes from all the very best restaurants in the city. One day we're actually going to eat in one of them. But until then, we like to walk into the fancy ones, pretend we're inspecting them for a dinner party, smile and leave with their matches.

"Lucija, not even Canadians give matches for presents."

"Mama!" I headed for the door. "There's *no way no how* I'm bringing flowers. Forget it. Jackie'll drop dead from laughing."

So . . . off I went dragging these stupid dahlias.

The flowers got pretty chewed up by the time I knocked on the door. Mrs. Lewis opened it, and a wall of perfume and cigarette smoke hit me in the face.

"Oh, how darling!" she smiled. "For me? You must be Lucy. Come in, dear."

Jackie charged up behind her. "Ha!" she sprayed. "Flowers! Now that's a first!"

My eyes were still smarting from the smells. Mrs. Lewis turned and floated into the kitchen. God, even her behind was stupendous. Movie stars don't look that good and she was a mom. For one thing, she had gigantic hair. Great big, puffy, silver-yellow hair that didn't move, at all, ever. And she had on tons and tons and tons of makeup. Her eyes were frosty, her lips were frosty and her cheeks were frosty. She was definitely the most beautiful, shimmering, sparkly person I had ever seen.

I mumbled a "You're welcome," but I don't think anyone actually thanked me for anything.

"Okay, sweeties," she said between puffs of her cigarette, stuffing the flowers in a vase, "you girls play nice until Carole finishes her shift at Loblaws." The smoke came out of her mouth in incredible jet streams. "I'm off. Ta. . . ." Mrs. Lewis floated back to the hallway. The door slammed and she was gone. Why? I wanted her to stay. I sniffed the air.

"Evening in Paris," said Jackie. "I think she puts too much on. Well, sit down. I hope you like Kraft Dinner because that's what I'm making."

"You're kidding," I gulped, "it's my favorite thing. Where did your mom go?"

"Oh," she shrugged, "she's on evenings for a while, ya know."

I didn't, but I nodded anyway. "Um, your mother—I've, uh, well, she's *so* . . ."

"Yeah, I know," said Jackie. "It's mainly the hair, don't you think? Platinum Moonlight, Clairol #221. The roots are a bitch, though."

"That must be it," I agreed. Roots?

"You'd be great as a blonde," she said. "I'll do you when you're older, okay? Grade eight, maybe. I do my mother. It'll be a gas."

"Wow, yeah, sure." I nodded. Do me? Blonde? I could be a blonde?

I helped her set the table. They had these beautiful green plastic plates.

"Karen . . . ! Kyle . . . !" she screeched. "Get your little butts up here! Dinner's ready." Two giggling blondes scrambled up from the basement. They looked like a Christmas card.

"Not Kraft again!" whined Karen.

"Shut up and eat," said Jackie.

I was on my third bowl when we heard Carole come in.

"Hi, kiddos!" she called.

"Great—Carole!" yelled Jackie. "Come here and meet my new friend, Lucy. She brought flowers. Too much, eh?"

Carole smiled at me. "Glad to meet you, Lucy. Any friend of my useless kid sister is a friend of mine."

Jackie jumped up to get her a clean plastic plate.

"No dinner for me, beanpole." Carole examined herself in the kitchen mirror. "Gotta watch my weight."

What a family! Carole was even more gorgeous than Mrs. Lewis. They all had the same sort of hair—extra blonde, Sandra Dee hair. God, I want to be Sandra Dee. I think Carole was wearing the same beige lipstick Sandra Dee wore in *A Summer Place,* a great movie.

She turned to me. "Nice flowers, kid. That was really sweet." I stood up. Should I shake her hand?

"Hey," she started at me, "you're a stunning little thing, aren't you?"

The smile freeze-dried on my face. Stunning! Wow! That's great—isn't it? Where does stunning fit in on the loveliness scale? You know nice is at the bottom, lovely is almost as bad, then there's cute, pretty, beautiful and finally gorgeous. Stunning, I don't know. It sounded good.

"Stunned is more like it," barked Jackie. "She's Italian."

"Croatian," I said. "But we've been here for a long time, years and years."

"Whatever," said Carole. She checked her watch. "You're still stunning. Look, guys, are you gonna be okay? I have to meet Johnny. It's really, really important."

"Ah jeez, Carole," whined Jackie. "What for? He's a jerk. You're supposed to stay here and—"

"Cool it!" Carole bit her lip and smiled at the same time. "Let's not go through this again, okay, please? Look, uh, why don't you guys come up and help me get ready, okay?"

"All right, all right, but Carole, can't you see? He's just—"

"Jackie!"

"All right already! I said all right, didn't I?"

We filed up behind Carole to her room.

You couldn't set a foot down without stepping on something. Bras, stockings, *Seventeen* magazines and eyebrow and lipstick pencils covered the floor. The two unmade twin beds were white with gold trim, and they exactly matched the dresser. It was beautiful.

Jackie threw herself on a bed. I carefully picked my way over, rearranged a heap of clothes and sat beside Jackie. I noticed a strange board game with underwear on it.

"What's that?" I pointed.

Carole looked over and smiled at it. "Hmmm. That's the Ouija Board. A bunch of us used to play with it in the basement all the time before. It's for contacting the other world. Beanpole was always sneaking down when she thought we were in trance." Jackie coughed. "It used to be such a gas."

Carole slipped out of her Loblaws uniform and kicked it to a corner of the room. Her bra and panties matched—baby blue underthings! Wow! Next she rifled through the dresser and grabbed a pair of fluorescent green fishnet stockings. She turned to Jackie.

"Hot pink or black?"

"Pink dress, black shoes," sighed Jackie.

The dress was shorter than the top I was wearing. Then Carole piled on love beads, bangles, an ankle bracelet and hoop earrings. She reapplied her beige lipstick and smothered herself with *Love's Freshscent Lemon* perfume. We all got up and stared at the image in the dresser mirror.

"The August issue of *Seventeen* says that when a lady thinks she is perfect and ready to go, she removes one item of jewelry," said Carole. "Only then will she be truly elegant." Off went the ankle bracelet. "Perfect?"

"Perfect," we nodded.

Honk. HONK. Carole stiffened. Jackie stood up and blocked the doorway.

"Make him come in," she said.

"Jackie . . . he's just—"

"Make—him—come—in," she said. "A gentleman comes to the door for his lady. That was in the October issue. You're a lady, aren't you, Carole?"

HON–N–N–K.

"Jackie . . ." She bit her lip again, no smile.

We heard the front door fly open. We all rushed to the top of the stairs.

"Johnny?"

"Carole? What gives?" He was cute, like page-forty-three-of-the-Eaton's-catalog cute. "Get your ass down here. Are ya deaf?" He stared at us staring at him. "Who's the wop?" She didn't answer. Instead, Carole flew downstairs and flicked butterfly kisses all over his Upper Canada College jacket. "Sorry, Johnny."

"I'm going to barf," muttered Jackie.

Johnny disentangled himself. "Let's go, eh? The gang's at the Ghost. Let's move."

Carole shrank. She turned to look up at Jackie. "Beanpole?"

"Yeah, I'll cover for you when Mom calls." Jackie sat on the landing. "But be back in time for *Gunsmoke,* okay?"

"Sure thing." She giggled and whispered to Johnny. He rolled his eyes. The door slammed and they were gone.

"Jerk," spat Jackie. "Rosedale jerk."

"What does Rosedale mean?"

"It means you're stinking rich," she said. "It means you live in a big house. It means you're a jerk."

She ran down the stairs and swung open a cupboard. "Okay, dessert time!" She flung some clear plastic packages onto the table. Inside each package were two large, perfectly round cookies. I watched Karen and Kyle before I tore through the plastic with my teeth.

"These are fabulous," I said. "Who made them?"

"They're just Dad's," she shrugged.

"But I thought your father—"

"Not *my* dad, goof. *Dad's!*" She grabbed a bright yellow box from the cupboard. *"Dad's Oatmeal Cookies.* Don't they have cookies where you come from?"

"Yes—I mean, no, I mean, not store cookies. Mama bakes them."

"Unbelievable," she said. "She bakes? Nobody bakes. At least not my mother. At least not so I can remember. Carole says Mom used to bake sometimes. Before . . . well, she doesn't anymore. Maybe I could try some sometime, eh?"

"Well, I—"

"Great, when? How about Jenny and Cindy, too? We can all come over after school one day."

Oh God. My house? Mama? "Maybe some Monday or Wednes—"

"Let me check my calendar." She strolled back in the room, examining a hacked-up Barbie diary.

"Got it! Two weeks Tuesday. Mom goes on days then, and I won't have to baby-sit."

"Sure," I said. "Can't wait," I said.

We cleaned up. That was okay except I'd never seen a dishwasher before. I also helped her put Karen and Kyle to bed. That was nice. We talked a lot, I guess. Jackie went on about Carole and what stupid jerks boys were, especially Johnny.

I had to agree.

"He treats her like dirt, cheap dirt."

"He can't do that!" I said. "She's a Canadian and she's so beautiful, exactly like Sandra Dee."

"Yeah?" said Jackie. "You think so? You should've told her. She loves Sandra Dee. She's seen *Gidget* five times. She used to be such a gas." Jackie shook her head. "But he makes her weird. Like last week when he stood her up for the hundredth time. She just went upstairs and stayed there. I think she went to bed before eight o'clock. Then she wakes up after midnight and spends the rest of the evening barfing in the can and crying."

We swore we'd never have boyfriends. At eight-thirty, I thanked Jackie and said good-night. I shuffled through every pile of leaves all the way down Cleveland Street. It wasn't even November and most of the leaves had fallen. I bet winter comes to Cleveland Street before it gets to Bathurst Street.

I thought about Carole all the way home. It was all so different from how I thought it was going to be. I don't know how exactly, but it was.

I kissed Mama and ran to the bathroom mirror. For an hour and half, I tried a thousand different poses. I turned my head just so, this way, then that. I raised my eyebrows, sucked in my cheeks, smiled mysteriously. . . . It was no use, though. I just couldn't find the look, the one that made me stunning.

Chapter Four

"Now *remember,* Mama," I warned, "don't improvise."

See, Jackie, Cindy and Jenny were all coming over after dinner. Mama baked for three nights straight. I kept explaining about how important it was not to look overeager. "Nonchalant, Mama, nonchalant." She nodded and smiled at me between batches.

We rehearsed her English for days. The deal was that Mama was supposed to come into the living room and say in a real soft voice, "Hello, girls. How lovely to meet you all. Perhaps you would care for a cookie?" Then she would place the cookies on the coffee table, smile and leave. She'd spend the rest of the time in the kitchen pretending to read *A Tale of Two Cities* by Charles Dickens. He's from England. I borrowed it from the library at Emily McDonald's.

"Oh, and remember I've changed our name," I reminded her. "We don't say Vook-o-veech anymore, it's Vak-o-vik."

"Okay, okay," she muttered. "It sounds just as immigrant to me, but you *want* Vakovik, we'll *be* Vakovik."

The doorbell rang. I raced to get it. It was Cindy and Jackie. "Hi, guys," I said, real cool like. While they were taking off their coats and things, Jenny came tripping up the porch steps.

"I like your door," she said.

"Uh, thanks," I said. "We're thinking of getting it painted. Blue maybe."

"Blue's nice," said Cindy.

"Hey!" called Jackie from the living room. "Where the Hell is the dining room? Whose bed is this?"

"Oh . . ." God. I forgot about that. Regular Canadians have dining room furniture in their dining rooms. "Mine," I whispered. I was going to die. No, I was dying. How *could* I forget about dining rooms? They all have dining room furniture, dining room tables, dining room chairs, dining room china cabinets. I had a double bed and a dresser. They didn't even match.

"That's neat," she said, "you can see the TV from your bed."

"Yeah," I snorted, "it's great."

Just then Mama burst in with a huge platter of cookies, five different assortments. "Halloo everybodies, halloo! Nice to be lovely to meeting my lovely Lucija's lovely friends . . . is lovely."

Everyone gasped. You'd think she could get one lousy little sentence right.

"Wow, jeez!" they erupted at once.

"Did you make all those cookies, Mrs. Vakovik?" asked Jenny.

"I've seen bakeries with less stuff in them," said Jackie.

"Pa-da!" smiled Mama. "You be 'scusing my sometime English is broking."

Oh God . . . she was ad-libbing. If only they could speak Croatian. Mama is so good in Croatian.

"I be baking dis lovely cookies for visiting to making nice." She beamed at me. "You van it nice to drink someting? Eating, too? I got kolbasa, bread, milk, I getting 'na frige?"

"Milk, please," said Cindy.

"Me, too, please," nodded Jenny.

"What's a kolbasa?" asked Jackie.

"Come," Mama held out her hand, "I showing you 'na kitchen." Mama and Jackie came back with milk and meat.

This was all wrong and they were just pretending not to notice. Canadians don't sit around munching on kolbasa and almond mocha cookies. I had to think of something. "Have I ever told you . . ." I said, "that . . . my great, great, great grandmother was an Iroquois Indian?"

"Get outta here! No way!" scoffed Jenny.

"No guff," I insisted, "I am actually one-eighth pure, adulterated, real, native Canadian."

"You mean one-eighth pure adultery," interrupted Jenny.

"No," said Cindy, "adultery has something to do with sex."

"It's pure *un*adulterated," groaned Jackie.

"Yeah, anyway . . ." I plugged on, "the Indian heritage gets passed down through the women, just like Jewishness. I'm full of Indian features like . . . like all Iroquois have uh . . . well . . . browny-black, black eyes. Not just regular brown eyes. Look at mine." I blinked at everyone. "See, these are Iroquois eyes."

"Well . . ." Jenny examined me carefully, "they're real dark all right."

"Sure," I nodded, "that's why Mama makes me wear braids and stuff."

"That's so neat," said Cindy. "We don't have anything interesting in our family, except my mother's grandmother was Welch."

"That's a grape juice, genius." Jackie rolled her eyes. Jenny giggled and I continued blinking at everyone. Jackie stared at me. "Your mom's unbelievable," she said. "We wouldn't even get this at Christmas. Do you think that, maybe, I could bring a couple of cookies home? You know, for Karen and Kyle and, well, really for Carole. She loves cookies. Maybe cookies would snap her out of it. She's starting to spook me, she's so bugged out."

"Men," sighed Jenny. We all nodded wisely.

I was so relieved that she didn't want to know what an Iroquois princess was doing coming from Zagreb, that I would have given her the whole platter. "Sure!" I said. "Cookies for everyone!" I ran to the kitchen and yelled at Mama to put the book down and make up gift packages. She tried to give me a hug, but I escaped. "Done!" I announced back in the living room.

"Thanks," smiled Jackie. "Okay, you guys, I have something to tell you. You know how we decided not to go out for Halloween?" Everyone nodded. I nodded—I didn't know what we were nodding about. "Well, it sort of leaves a hole, doesn't it? We need something. So . . . I have found it. I have found our clubhouse!"

"Clubhouse?" asked Jenny. "What for?"

"For our club, you goof!" barked Jackie. "We're going to form a secret club, the Tomcats. You know the laneway behind Davisville?" We all nodded again. "Well, the third garage in from Bayview on the left-hand side is empty. Old lady Marshall lives there. She doesn't have a car and she never leaves the house. That garage will be our clubhouse. We'll be mutually exclusive."

"What's that?" asked Cindy.

"It means just us, stupid," said Jackie. "The whole school will be our minions. That means slaves."

"So how's that different from now?" Jenny just didn't know when to shut up. I'd seen this before when, for no reason, Jackie would rip into everything Jenny said or did. Cindy said it was like that since kindergarten. I guess Jenny didn't notice.

"Because, runt," Jackie glared at her, "we'll be a club! We're gonna be invincible. We'll have initiation and everything. That's a test, a test of loyalty—to prove you're worthy. I haven't figured out all the details yet. I'll work it all through for Susan Ambrose's birthday party. That's on November thirteenth. Yeah, I'll have it all figured out by then."

"Sounds great!" said Cindy.

"Yeah," nodded Jenny.

Party? What party? Well, who cares? Not me. I didn't want to go to a stupid party. I examined the ceiling and thought about my Iroquois heritage.

"What are you going to wear, Lucy? I made her invite you, too. You want to go, don't you?"

"You're kidding!" I bounced on the sofa. "Sure. Yeah. God, yeah."

We all agreed that, since we were eleven and everything, we would *not* wear party dresses. This was good since I didn't have one.

"So what do you want to be when you grow up?" asked Jackie. "You know, when I was a kid, I wanted to be a hairdresser. But now I think that sucks and I've decided I'd rather be a movie star."

"Yeah," nodded Jenny. "When I was a kid, I wanted to be a vet, but now I want to be a movie star, too."

"Yeah," agreed Cindy. "When I was a kid, I wanted to be a teacher, but now I want to be a movie star, too, but the kind that are on the TV soaps."

"Yeah," I nodded. "Well, I've got a really dumb one. See, when I was a kid, I wanted to be a mermaid. Isn't that a riot? But now I really, really want to be a writer." Silence. No one nodded.

"Jeez, Lucy," said Jackie, "I don't know which one is dumber to tell you the truth."

"Yeah." Everyone nodded.

"Well . . ." My stomach twisted and untwisted. "What I *mean* is that . . . I mean . . . I want to be an actor–writer. Like I'd write in all the best parts for me. And my friends, I mean."

"Oh, okay," said Jackie. "That's cool!"

"Yeah!" nodded Jenny and Cindy.

We talked a bit more about what glamorous people we'd all be, and then they left. I pressed my face against the living-room window and watched them hip-checking one another down Cleveland Street. When they disappeared I ran to the phone.

"Hi, Emily? So how are you?"

"Lucy?"

"Yeah, it's me, Lucy. Look, Emily, are you going to Susan Ambrose's birthday party? Because I am."

"Oh, super! We can go together. That's great, Lucy. Susan has the best birthday parties."

"Yeah, well, I guess. Uh, Emily, what do you guys buy for each other, you know, for presents?"

"Oh . . . I see. . . . Well, I was going to get her a new Barbie."

"A Barbie?"

"Yeah, listen, she *collects* them. She's got the world's largest collection. Only she's always complaining that no one buys them for her anymore because she's too old."

"Oh. . . ."

"Look, Lucy, you go to Eaton's and buy her a Barbie. I guarantee she'll love it. I'll think of something else for me to get."

"Jeez. Thanks, Emily. You're a pal. Look, I'll meet you there because it's market day, but we'll walk back together, okay?"

"Sure, super. See you in the morning. Bye."

"Mama!" I yelled to the kitchen.

She came booming out, arms outstretched. "Did it go good? *I* think it went good. Do *you* think it went good?"

"Well, it sort of went good, bad, good, bad, great."

Mama stopped in her tracks.

"But see, the great part is that I'm going to Susan Ambrose's birthday party, and we have to buy a Barbie doll at Eaton's before November thirteenth. Isn't that great?"

"Did I do something bad?" she asked.

"No, Mama, no. You were . . . unbelievable."

She beamed.

"How many English classes have you had so far?" See, Mama's been going to night school at Northern Secondary every Thursday evening. English for New Canadians. She wasn't doing very well.

"Four," she said. "Why?"

"It shows," I lied. "You're doing much better, but maybe a little more practice, huh? Maybe we should talk in English together once a week or something. Like, every Friday could be an English-only day."

"Yah, yah. What was the bad part, Lucija?" Mama put her arm around me.

We walked back into the kitchen. "Oh, I don't know Mama," I shrugged. "I blew it when we were talking about what we want to be when we grow up. I think I keep breaking a bunch of rules."

"You keep telling me about the rules here, Lucija," she frowned. "What *are* the rules?"

"That's the problem, Mama, I just don't know."

Chapter Five

$\mathcal{W}$e argued about the Barbie the whole time we cleaned Taylor, Laidlaw and Abromovitz. It was Saturday, November thirteenth. The day of the party and we still hadn't bought the stupid Barbie.

"Mama, we've *got* to buy it at Eaton's," I said for the hundredth time. "Emily said to buy it at Eaton's."

"It costs $6.93 at Eaton's," she said. "We're going to Honest Ed's."

"We *can't* buy it there," I whined. "All the poor people in the whole planet go to Honest Ed's. Susan will know. How about Simpson's? Simpson's is even better."

"It cost $6.27 at Simpson's," she said, emptying a garbage can. "We're going to Honest Ed's."

"You're not even listening." I hopped onto the conference table. "Canadians do not buy their stuff at Honest Ed's. I'll be humiliated. Uh-uh. This is my first one hundred percent all-Canadian birthday party, and I am *not* bringing an Honest Ed's Barbie. No way. Uh-uh."

The Barbie was on sale for $4.50 at Honest Ed's. We also bought three pairs of socks and a lime green ski jacket for me. Okay, so it looked just like the Eaton's Barbie, but there was probably some invisible code or something that everyone else would see.

38

I've been going to Honest Ed's all of my life, and I still can't find my way out of there. For one thing, no matter when you go, there's always three million people in with you, trying to buy exactly the same thing you are. For another, the store is set up like a snakes and ladders game. You can wander around and around and up and down and still always end up in the men's underwear section.

Mama and I were shoving our way through today's three million shoppers on our way to the checkout when I saw her by the pharmacy section. The extra blonde hair. Oh God, Carole Lewis!

I tried to duck behind an Italian family in front of us. It looked like Carole was trying to blend into a bunch of Koreans. No use. I saw her. She saw me. Finally, we both stood still and stared at each other across the floor. Carole was hanging onto a package from the pharmacy. She hugged it tighter, smiled just a little and put her finger to her lips. Then she vanished.

I decided not to say anything to Mama. Her being there smelled like a secret. Yeah. Maybe it would be our secret. Maybe, if I didn't tell, she wouldn't tell. It would just be for us, a Carole–Lucy thing. Yeah. Yeah, but why in the world would Carole come to Honest Ed's of all places?

The party was from 3:30 to 6:30 p.m. At 3:35 I knocked on the door. Mrs. Ambrose and Susan answered the door together. The whole way over I worried about the hello part. Do you say, "How do you do? Thank you for inviting me." Then shake hands, then hand over the present? Or do you shake hands right away, then say, "Hello," or, well, you know. I managed to do all three at once without screwing it up.

She was beige. Mrs. Ambrose, I mean. She wore a

beige sweater set on top of a beige and brown checked skirt. Her hair and shoes were beige, too . . . peach lipstick, though.

"Mother," Susan smiled. "This is Lucy Vakovik. Jackie says that Lucy's mother bakes."

"I'm sure she does, dear." Mrs. Ambrose smiled, but her face got all pointy. "Va–ko–vik, my! What kind of name is that, dear? It sounds foreign. Vakovik. I'm sure I've never heard anything quite so, well, exotic."

"She was born in Zagreb, Mrs. Ambrose. That's in Europe, you know." Emily McDonald had slipped in behind me. "Don't mind her," she whispered. "Well, we're all here now, Susan. Is it present time?"

"Oh yes!" bounced Susan. "Can we, Mother?"

"Of course," said Mrs. Ambrose. She was still examining me. "Shall we?" she pointed to the back of the house.

"Shall we what?" I asked.

"Come on." Emily took my arm and we walked through three different rooms, not including the kitchen.

"God," I whispered to Emily, "they've got *two* living rooms. Wait till I tell Mama." All the kids were sitting in the second living room.

"No," Emily smiled. "This is called a family room. They put on an addition five years ago."

"Hey, Lucy," Jackie called, patting a sofa seat beside her. "I saved you a spot."

"Uh," I looked at Emily. "She sort of got me invited."

"Yeah," she shrugged.

I had never seen so many presents in one place before. It was too beautiful. Most of the bows exactly matched the wrapping paper. Mine was the smallest present. It didn't have a bow. There was barely enough room to stick the card on. Actually, the card was bigger than the present.

"I lost the bow on the way over," I said to the room.

Susan's parents gave her a pink and white record player. I wondered if they were going to replace the big wooden hi-fi set in their first living room.

"It's for her room, stupid," said Jackie.

"Wow."

She got two huge Crayola art sets, a Pretty in Pink, Young Miss Makeup Set by Avon, a white angora sweater. Emily bought her three *Nancy Drew* books. Jackie bought a Monopoly game. Jenny gave her Scrabble. Cindy gave her a hook-your-own rug craft thing. She also got a box full of psychedelic leotards from Lisa Kirkland. Her father makes them. She almost didn't see mine.

"Oh, and what's this?" she said, grabbing my big card, small box, no bow. She opened the card. "It's from *Lucy*. How sweet!" She tore at the paper. "Oh God."

I waited for bells to go off and colored lights to flash: Honest Ed's! Honest Ed's!

"Awww . . ." she squealed. "It's a Barbie! Oh, thank you, thank you. It's my favorite present. Really. Thanks Lucy."

"I'm glad you like it." I beamed and looked at Emily. She gave me thumbs up.

"Okay, ladies!" Mrs. Ambrose clapped her beige hands. "Shall we adjourn to the dining room for refreshments?"

We stampeded through her to the food. Absolutely everything was pink and white. Pink and white streamers, balloons, paper plates, paper cups, and a pink and white paper tablecloth. Mama would have probably ruined everything by sticking an embroidered linen job on the dining room table. If we had a dining room table.

Emily ripped a bit of the tablecloth as she sat down. In fact, the tablecloth was pretty well in shreds by the time we finished our Cheezies. Then Mrs. Ambrose waltzed in with a huge platter of sandwiches. *"Ta da!"*

"Oooh!" we all gasped.

The sandwiches were pink and white! They were gorgeous. They were done like little pinwheels. The pink bread had white swirls with a Maraschino cherry in the middle, and the white bread had pink swirls with a pickle in the middle.

I took four of each and wolfed down a pink and white one. I gagged. God. It was awful. So was the white and pink one. It was like eating the tablecloth.

I looked around. Nobody was eating. "What *is* this stuff?" I asked Jackie.

"Gross, eh?" she laughed. "It's all cream cheese or dyed cream cheese, but you have to freeze that stuff to keep those shapes. Yuk. I always load up on peanut butter before I come here."

The cake was pink and white. You had to crunch through sugar granules in the icing. "She should have had your mom do the catering," muttered Jackie.

For the last hour, we all traipsed up to Susan's pink and white bedroom to play some records on her new record player and dance. Everyone wanted to dance with Jackie. She was amazing. I loved to watch her. I didn't know people could move that way. I danced two fast dances with her and one each with Emily and Jenny. Just before leaving, Susan and I danced to "God Don't Make Little Green Apples."

"I'm real glad you came, Lucy," she smiled at me, "and I really, really do love the Barbie."

"Yeah," I nodded, "but she's got that blue dress on . . . sorry . . . I didn't know about you and, well, I should have bought the one with the pink dress."

"No!" she shook her head. "I love blue; it's my favorite color."

I will *never* understand these people.

As soon as Emily and I got outside, I noticed Jackie, Jenny and Cindy near the corner. Jackie turned and ran over to us.

"Great party, eh?" said Emily.

"Give me a break," said Jackie. "Look, Emily, I need to talk to Lucy here about club business, private-like. So do you think you can manage to find your own way home?"

Emily turned instant tomato red. "Uh, sure, of course. Look, Lucy, we'll, uh, get together tomorrow or, well, maybe tomorrow." She smiled at me. No dimple.

"Yeah, tomorrow's good, yeah." Jackie grabbed my arm and started pulling me down the street.

"Jackie, that wasn't very . . . you know. I don't see why Emily can't belong to our—"

"Get real!" she said. "This is a club for Tomcats, not Girl Scouts. You watch who you hang out with."

That did it, almost. "I'll hang out with whoever I want, and it's Girl *Guides*, not Scouts!"

"Okay, okay," she waved her hand. "Girl Sucks if you ask me, and Emily's one of the biggest." We reached Jenny and Cindy.

"Okay, guys," she said, "I've got it. I've worked it all out. Each of you will have to pass an initiation test on Monday. If you do it, you're in. You're a Tomcat for life. Okay?"

"Yeah, okay, sure." We all nodded.

"Good," she said. "Lucy, if you want to be in, you

have to do something to really shake up Old Gladbags. Any problems?"

"To Mrs. Glad?" I sort of liked her, a lot. "No, no problem. I can, uh, yeah . . . okay, sure."

"Good." She smiled. "These two'll carry out their test together. We'll all meet at the clubhouse at 4:15 sharp."

"Why not at 3:45?" asked Cindy.

Jackie shook her head. "Because Monday is Carole's day to baby-sit. Only, like, she's never ever around lately. It's really pissing me off, you know."

I remembered Carole at the Honest Ed's pharmacy. I felt my face burn, but I just nodded with everyone else.

Mama was waiting at the door. *"So . . . ?"* she said.

"It was great, Mama. I did great; the Barbie was great. It was all great. Except, except, it looked so–o–o–o beautiful but, but—I don't know how to explain it. You wouldn't understand."

Mama smiled. "Want some kolbasa?"

There! You see! While I was changing and turning into a real Canadian, she was getting more immigrant by the minute.

"Yes, please, Mama," I said. "A big piece. I'm starving."

Chapter Six

I spent all of Saturday worrying about what to do to Mrs. Glad. I mean, whatever I did, it had to be very secret and pretty awful. By the time Emily McDonald and I started for school on Monday, I had it. I didn't like it much, but I had it.

"Um, Emily, uh, sorry, but I can't come over after school today," I said. "Something has come up."

"Oh. Well. Oh." She looked at my shoes. "How about tomorrow? Tomorrow would be just as good. We could finish our mystery book. Or . . . or not."

I hated that. It made me twitchy when she was so understanding. "Yeah," I said. "Sure."

I was going to do what I had to do in the morning, but I couldn't do it. All through recess, I kept nodding and winking at Jackie, Jenny and Cindy. "Just you wait!" I said. "Just you wait!"

Well, they had to wait some more because I couldn't do it after recess either. I really was going to do it right after lunch, but Mrs. Glad was already in a real muddle. Someone had broken into the teachers' lounge and made off with all the staff lunches. She'd have to calm down before I muddled her up some more, or else it wouldn't count.

At afternoon recess Jackie cornered me at the swings. "Well?"

"Just you wait." I smiled and nodded. Oh God.

2:45 p.m. Okay, okay—less than one hour left. Better do it, get to it. 3:00 p.m. Here I go. . . . I was the last one in the last row. Easy, no problem. I had some matches from Mama's matchbox collection. Okay, okay, 3:10 p.m. The wastebasket was right behind me. So-o-o-o . . . so maybe I didn't really need to be a Tomcat after all. I could find other friends. We could do interesting stuff. Yeah! . . . There was Emily. . . .

3:15 p.m. No,. I really, really needed to be a Tomcat. Jackie and them, well, they were *it* at Maurice Cody. I *had* to be part of *it*. Didn't I? 3:25 p.m. You'd think a class of twenty-eight would make more noise. Jackie shot me a look.

3:30 p.m. My stomach turned over. This is it. I started to cough, turned around, struck the match— and threw it in the wastebasket. Bingo! It took! A flame. There was flame! I turned back to face the front of the room. Emily was looking at me, staring at me. Nobody else noticed a thing, but nothing! My heart was exploding in my chest. 3:32 p.m. Mary, Mother of God, the entire school was going to be shot down in flames! I was going to burn in Hell forever, and the rest of Room 501 kept copying out homework questions!

3:35 p.m. It was blazing. 3:36 p.m. "Mrs. Glad?" I croaked. "I smell fire."

"Aeaagh! The wastebasket!" someone screamed. The school bell rang. Time to go home. More screaming.

"Calm *down*, for Heaven's sake," snapped Mrs. Glad. "The wastebasket is made of heavy steel. Please file out quietly and go home. Lucy, dear, go outside to the hall, open the fire box door and bring me the fire extinguisher."

I tore out, shoving my way past kids craning for a

better look. I ran to the box, opened it on my third try and raced back with the fire extinguisher.

"Thank you, dear," she smiled and whooshed white foam into the can. 3:45 p.m. It was out. Everyone was gone.

Mrs. Glad turned to me and cupped my face in her hands.

"You have such a remarkable head on your shoulders, Lucy, dear." My stomach began to twist. "You could do so many splendid things with such a remarkable head."

My remarkable head was going to burst. She knew! My God, she knew. And not only did she know, but she knew that I knew that she knew.

"Yes, Mrs. Glad," I squirmed. "Thank you, ma'am."

"You're welcome, dear," she said. "I'll see you tomorrow."

I held my breath and listened to her heels click farther and farther down the hall. That was it! I did it! Great. Super—right?

Somehow I was on Cleveland Street, walking toward the clubhouse. I crossed Davisville Avenue and was about to turn into the laneway when I saw Emily. She was standing on the corner of Cleveland and Balliol.

"Lucy!" she called. "Hi! You okay? I just wanted to be sure. I mean, Mrs. Glad—she didn't . . . ?"

"No." I threw up my hands. "It's okay. Really."

"Lucy, don't worry. I'd *never* tell, you know. *Never.* Okay?"

"Yeah." I pointed toward the lane. "I have to, uh . . ."

"Yeah." She nodded and walked away.

I wanted to run after her so bad. I wanted to explain or finish the mystery book, or *something*.

I went to the clubhouse.

"Great fire!" screamed Jenny as soon as she saw me. *"Out*standing!"

"I bet you really freaked out old Gladbags," giggled Cindy.

"You bet," I said. "She was a mess all right."

"You want a ham and cheese sandwich?" asked Jenny. "I think it's Mr. Hoffman's."

I laughed, finally laughed. I couldn't stop laughing. "So it *was* you guys! What a day!" We congratulated each other and went on about how brilliant we were. No one could touch us. We were Tomcats. We were bulletproof.

I looked around our clubhouse. "Hey," I said, "this place is a dump. It needs some stuff." Jenny and Cindy were sitting on upturned garbage cans. "You know, it looks like . . . well, like a garage."

"Yeah," nodded Cindy, "we were talking about it. I'm going to bring in a bunch of my sister's old Janis Joplin posters, and Jenny's got a broken wheelbarrow we can turn into a table, and maybe Jackie—"

"Where is Jackie, anyway?" I asked.

"She always has to go home first to check things out." Jenny shrugged. "Either Carole or her mom is probably having another little crisis. They've flooded the toilet four times this year already."

"Yeah, they're always having a little crisis," nodded Cindy. "She'll turn up."

But she didn't. We waited and waited. At 5:15, we went home, giggling and hooting.

Jackie didn't come to school the next day. Or the next.

And Friday, well, Friday it wasn't a little crisis.

It was worse than any crisis.

Carole was dead.

Chapter Seven

On Tuesday right after school, I went back to St. Raymond's. I must have taken the bus, the subway and the streetcar, but I don't remember. I remember I wanted to light some candles for Carole, and St. Anselm's, our new church, didn't have any, but St. Raymond's did. So somehow I was standing in front of those ancient carved doors.

You'd think with something so huge, you'd have to heave and yank at the handle. But St. Raymond's doors swing open with barely a pull and you're in. Five little old ladies wearing black lace head scarves were scattered throughout empty pews. They looked familiar. They were probably there all the times I ever was. Maybe they never left. The light was the same, not dark, but soft and gentle. It was good to be home.

I headed straight for the candles, put a quarter in the box, picked up the wick and lit the big yellow one in the very middle. I didn't want her to be lonely.

Hail Mary full of Grace.

Carole had gone and killed herself!

The Lord is with you.

She was actually dead.

Blessed art thou amongst women.

She stayed at home yesterday and did it.

And blessed is the fruit of thy womb Jesus.

49

I shouldn't have set the fire.

Holy Mary, Mother of God.

She swallowed a whole bottle of some of Mrs. Lewis's medicine. That's what Jenny's mother said. She killed herself with medicine.

Pray for us sinners.

Carole! You look exactly like Sandra Dee. Exactly. Why didn't I tell her? That's what I should have told her.

Now and at the hour of our death.

I'm sorry. I don't understand anything, not a thing . . . stupid, stupid, stupid.

Amen.

Chapter Eight

*W*e were pretty well the only ones wearing black at the funeral. Mama made me wear the black knit dress we bought two years ago for Buba Meekleech's funeral. It was way too short and the sleeves barely got past my elbows. I felt like an elegant gorilla.

Everyone wore black at Buba Meekleech's funeral. Mama says that in Bili Brig—that's where she was born—the whole village wears black all the time. See, as soon as someone in your family drops dead, that's it, *boom*, you're in black forever. Mama still can't get over all the colors in Canada.

Carole was *resting* at the Humphrey Funeral Home at Bayview and MacRae. *Resting*—what a stupid word for it. Like she's going to get up and go shopping or something. She was dead and she wasn't going anywhere, ever. Mama couldn't get over that they weren't having the service in a church. "I know deese people getting lotsa churches." The funeral was on Friday, our English-only day. "Dis is 'na 'Home.' You tinking dis counts? I don't tinking dis counts."

I wasn't sure either. "Of course it counts, Mama," I said. "They know what they're doing." Buba Meekleech's service was at Our Lady, Queen of Croatia Catholic Church.

"I don't know dis counts," she shook her head.

It was a very pretty place, the funeral home. From the hallway part, you could see these really gorgeous rooms. The most beautiful one had this happy yellow wallpaper with pink and green flowers that you could actually feel. As it turned out, we weren't supposed to be in there feeling the wallpaper. A worried-looking usher came and got us. He took us to a teeny little room that said Chapel. It had wooden pews and everything.

"See, Mama," I said. "It's sort of like a church."

As soon as he sat us down, I had to get right back up and run after Mama. "Mama, come back here!" I whispered loudly. She'd gone back to the hallway and was looking around for the holy water basin.

"It's no use looking; they don't *have* holy water!" I took her arm. The same poor usher led us back to the same spot. It was just like a wedding except no one asked if you were on the groom's or the bride's side.

The Lewises sat in the very front. Mrs. Lewis wore a blue suit with little dots all over it. Jackie wore a brown turtleneck and brown corduroy skirt that she wears to school all the time. Karen and Kyle were too little for me to see. I kept trying to find someone who looked like the father. He would be tall and blond with blue eyes, and beautiful just like the rest of them. He wasn't there. Carole's boyfriend from Upper Canada College wasn't there either. I started to cry, which was seriously embarrassing. Absolutely nobody else was crying, not even the family.

A United Minister held the service. There was no communion, which really threw Mama. I had to explain all about Protestants again.

"There's different kinds," I whispered. "Some take communion all the time. Like the Queen, she takes it with a glass of wine. These people don't." She started to fret about Carole's immortal soul. *"Mama!"* I hissed. *"No* communion, *no* holy water, *no* church. Got it?" People were looking at us. Mama got all huffy.

We had barely sat down when it was all over. You know, maybe twenty minutes.

"Finish?" Mama was shocked. It takes Catholics an hour and a half to do anything. "No sing? I don't tinking dis counts."

"Shhh, Mama," I whispered. We all filed out quietly and drove over to the Mount Pleasant Cemetery. Mama and me went with Jenny and her parents. Nobody said anything.

At the cemetery, everyone stood politely around the hole. The United Church Minister said a few more Bible things. All the trees were bare and shivering. It was so cold, so gray and so very quiet. All of a sudden, it started to pour. Nobody moved. It was like they were all standing around waiting to get their picture taken. Finally, we all neatly followed the family back to the cars, two by two, in the rain. God was the only one crying.

At Buba Meekleech's cemetery you couldn't hear the priest for all the sobbing and wailing. Some of the family smeared grave dirt on their faces. Of course, it was summer then. Little old men blew their noses in handkerchiefs that looked like tablecloths. At least two old ladies that nobody even knew threw themselves on the coffin screeching and crying.

Buba Meekleech's party was good, too. It was held at the Hungarian Hall. The Croatian Hall was already booked for a christening. There were just hundreds of people packing their plates with cabbage rolls, roasted pork, bread. After dessert all us kids played hide-and-go-seek around the band equipment on stage. The women huddled in groups on one side of the hall. They sobbed and beat their chests moaning, *"Boze moj! Boze moj! Can you believe these cabbage rolls? So much rice you'd think Ukrainians did the catering."* Then they'd rock and sob some more.

The men sat on the other side bleary-eyed with their bottles of *Slivovic*. They spent the afternoon singing the Croatian National Anthem over and over and over again.

It was great.

Carole's party was going to be at her house. I guess it would've been stupid to rent a hall for so few people. On the way over, I reminded Mama not to say too much. "They probably won't talk or anything, but if they do, just smile sadly." She nodded. I knew she wouldn't listen. Mama never really listens. Sure enough, we barely got in the door when she marched right over to Mrs. Lewis and threw her arms around her. God!

"I am Mama for Lucija!" she wailed. "My heart is broking wit you for losing it your first baby!"

Well . . . instead of turfing her out, Mrs. Lewis grabbed onto Mama and began to sob! All her perfect makeup melted into frosted pink and blue streams that ran onto Mama's black dress.

I would have kept close tabs on them, but Jackie came up behind me and dug her nails into my arm. "Come to my room with me." Her voice was hoarse. Jenny was helping Karen and Kyle with their food. Uh-oh. Wait until Mama checked out the table. It was practically empty. There was a macaroni salad, some cold cuts and buns, and this big mound of green Jello with bits of marshmallows and fruit trapped inside. I glanced at Mama; she and Mrs. Lewis were glued together. I didn't want to go. It was Carole's room, too.

"Now!" Jackie hissed.

I trudged up the stairs behind her. She kicked her door shut and looked at the ceiling. "It was sleeping pills, you know," she said.

I didn't know. I didn't want to know. I asked anyway.

"What's that?"

"Nerve pills," she sighed. "Uppers or downers or something like that . . . my mother's."

Just like Marilyn Monroe. "Hey," I said. "Just like Marilyn Monroe. Thank God! Look, it'll be okay! It was an *accident*. Don't you see? She didn't mean it. That's real important. Her soul will be okay! Maybe a little time in purgatory, so we light a few candles, say a few prayers. Carole will not go to Hell!"

Jackie crumpled onto Carole's bed. "What are you talking about? Anyway, I don't know, maybe she did mean to . . . I . . . uh, I think she was pregnant. She kept running to the bathroom every five minutes to see if she started her . . . I don't know, I don't know. Remember how I told you about that one time she was crying and puking in the toilet all night?"

I shook my head.

"I, uh . . . found . . . uh . . . an empty bottle of Mom's old sleeping pill capsules and, uh . . . and . . . I didn't say a damn thing to anybody. Not Carole or Mom, nobody. Hell, she must have got a new prescription filled out somehow. The old bottle was hidden with all her makeup staff . . ."

I couldn't hear her anymore. A new prescription. Oh God, a new *prescription!*

No! I saw her smile, bite her lips. Shhh, our secret. "You're a *stunning* little thing." Carole in front of the mirror. "Perfect? Perfect." How could anyone who looked so–o–o–o do such . . . The room got wavy. "Excuse me." I ran to the bathroom and barely made it. I threw up, and threw up, and then threw up some more. A new prescription. If I'd only told about seeing her in Honest Ed's. I should've told her mom or Jackie or Father Mike or I don't know . . . someone. I washed up and felt my way back.

"Sorry," I said. "Uh, too much for breakfast given the excitement or just, just too much . . . Look, Jackie, we're in for some serious praying because . . ."

"I don't care about your goddamned breakfast or your Catholic crud! My sister is dead!" Finally, Jackie began to cry. Well, it was more like a howl or whooping cough. She scared me. I wanted to cry with her to make her feel less little, less alone, but there was nothing left. So I just held her. It felt real stupid, but I didn't let go.

After forever, Jackie stopped crying. She started hiccuping. "Thanks, *hic*. I'm okay, *hic*. Water, *hic.*" And then she ran to the bathroom. I sat on the floor. I didn't want to sit on her bed, and I sure wasn't going to sit on Carole's.

Jackie came back and stood in the doorway. She was holding a razor blade in her hand.

"Nothing will ever be the same again," she said.

"No," I nodded. "No, I guess it won't. What are you doing with that?"

"You and me, we're different." She sat down beside me. "I knew from the first day of class that you were like me. We're different and we're better and you know it, too."

"I am not different!" I said. "Look, I don't ever want to be different or better. I want to be just exactly like everyone else!"

"No." She smiled. "It's better to be better. Besides, we both know about not having fathers, and now I guess we both know about death."

"Well, not really," I said. "See, I was just a baby—"

"It's the same!" she hissed. "Dead is dead. We're like sisters really, and now we'll make it official. I'm going to slit my thumb right here, then yours; then we'll stick our blood together. Blood brothers for life, Lucy. D' you want to?"

I wanted to go home. "Yeah, sure," I said. "Great idea." She got real calm, slit her thumb and then . . . It hardly hurt, much. Jackie stared at me, or through me, right to Carole's makeup table. "Blood brothers for *life,* Lucy." Just then Mama yelled from the bottom of the stairs. "Lucija, time is going home."

"I've got to go." I jumped.

"Yeah," she nodded.

"You okay?"

"Yeah."

"Jackie, I'm real sorry. . . ."

"Yeah."

"Well, see you later."

"Yeah."

Downstairs, strangers were coming up to Mama and telling her how nice it was to meet her. She beamed at them all. Mr. and Mrs. Clarke invited us to dinner, some time soon. Mrs. Lewis hugged her hard. "Thank you, thank you for everything," she whispered. Karen and Kyle ran up to us waving. "Bye-bye, Mrs. V!"

Incredible! They loved her. Mama was the hit of the funeral! Go figure.

Chapter Nine

"That one's fifteen dollars," he said. I think he was the owner. Mama and me were at the Bayview Christmas Tree Center. We hadn't actually gotten around to thinking about the price, we were still arguing about the height in Croatian when he came up behind us. "Fifteen dollars," he repeated.

I turned around. He had brush-cut white hair and watery little blue eyes. He was wearing one of those weird ski jackets without any sleeves.

"No, no, no, you be tinking I meaning for all deese trees." Mama gave him her absolutely best smile. "I mean it really just deese little vu." She picked up the tree beside me.

"Well, see, lady," he squinted at Mama and his eye disappeared. "Maybe they're cheaper where you come from, but this here is a Canadian Christmas tree and it's *$15* just like it says on the tag. You understand about *dollars*, don't cha?"

Great! Mama looked like a volcano. Now she'd tear him limb from limb. There'd be a huge scene. We'd be banned from Bayview, and we still wouldn't have a Christmas tree!

Instead, she unsmiled herself, dropped the tree on his foot and stormed out of there. Away from him, away from the trees, away from *my* Christmas tree.

"Mama! Wait!" I screamed, running after her.

It was just four days until Christmas, and we still didn't have a tree.

See, we'd never had a tree. None of the landladies ever allowed it. But this Christmas, it was *our* house. This Christmas, *we* were the landladies.

"Mama! I know he's a jerk, but a tree, a Christmas tree. Please, Mama. You promised!" I didn't know anyone could walk so fast without breaking into a run. "*Mama*, remember we're supposed to be cheering me up. You know, Carole and everything? Mama! Where are we going?"

"To bus!" she yelled in English. "Vee going 'na Jewish market." She glared back at the Bayview Christmas Tree Center. "Dey getting better tree, not full of desease like doze place."

"Oh. Oh, okay then." I quit sniffling. That was okay. The Jewish market had trees.

We didn't stop for vegetables or cheese. We barely even said hello to the Jamaican lady who sold the Chinese chickens. Mama was still on fire. She thundered right over to Mr. Goldman's Kosher Meat Market. He had four thousand Christmas trees crammed into the space where he usually parked his trucks. As soon as Mr. Goldman saw us walk by the front window, he hurried out to the back.

"*Shalom, Shalom,* Madame Vookovich," he called.

"Ya!" Mama sighed and looked at him. "Same to you, Meester Goldman. I promise a tree dis year." She smiled. "Lucija, vitch vun you van it?"

I ran from tree to tree in a daze. "This one. No— that one! No—look, this one. No, no, oh—look! This one. Mama, this one, *please!*" It was a movie-star tree. You know, with short little needles, but real big and real fat. "Please, please."

"How much dis be costing?" she frowned.

"Such a smart kid," said Mr. Goldman. "She getting my best tree." He paused. "But, for you, such a good customer—seven dollar."

"Seven dollar!" Mama gasped and clutched at her heart. This was all right. I understood this. Mr. Goldman would never let me leave without my tree. I waited.

"Mrs. *Kostakis* got dem for tree dollar," Mama sniffed.

"Mrs. Kostakis!" he waved his hand. "Please, she's a Greek. Vat does a Greek know from Christmas trees? Dey vas cut in April. Da tree da kid vants vas cutting dis morning."

"Okay, tree-fifty," Mama sighed. "Not a penny more giving."

"Tree-fifty! You insulting my family." His hat fell off.

"You got it nice familja. How your son is being?" asked Mama. "Tree seventy-five. I got to buying kid present."

"Praise be God, he is a medical school now." He put his hat back on. "You got a knife in my heart. Okay, okay. Four dollar just for Lucija."

"You is stealing me, Meester Goldman," Mama shook her finger at him. "Na . . . Doctor school is cost big money. Okay, okay. Four dollar you be having merry Hanukah."

"I got such a blooding heart. I gonna trow in dis unbelievable tree stand. No fuss, no boddering." He nailed the tree stand on. "I'm stupid for vidow ladies. You be having happy Christmas."

I jumped up and kissed his sandpaper cheek.

"Go vay!" he blushed. "Such a princess."

It was mine! It was great! It was big, really big. How were we going to get it home?

"Lucija." Mama paused and switched back to Croatian. "Here, you take my purse and grab the pointy part." She hauled up the heavy end like it was nothing, and off we went. You should've seen the driver's face as we crammed that thing through the street-car doors. I didn't care. Some kids on the subway hooted at us. So what? The Davisville bus driver wanted to charge us extra, and Mama had to stare him down.

We got back by noon. Mama put the Christmas tree in front of the window. The tree made itself at home right away, and the whole house smelled like a forest. The Onlyhouse would protect it. No one would take it away. It belonged.

I absolutely had to call someone. Emily? Yeah! What with the funeral and Tomcat business, we barely saw each other. She was getting a permanently hurt look on her face when we walked to school. No. Yeah! Only Emily would understand about the tree.

"Hello?"

"Hi!" I said. "So how are you Emily?"

"Lucy? It's been so long I barely recognized your voice."

This was going to take a bit of work. But Emily was Emily.

"That's just great," she said after I told her about my perfect tree. "Do you have tons of decorations?"

"Decorations. Right." My heart sank. Regular people don't have bare naked Christmas trees. "Well," I scrambled, "Jackie gave me a bunch of construction paper."

"You mean the packs she hauled from the art supply room?"

"No, I mean, I don't know where she got them, really."

"Lucy, I know it's none of my business, but those guys are—"

"So anyway I figure I can make miles of paper chain links! What do you think?"

"Yeah, sure, paper chains can be very pretty. A nice color repeat maybe." I bet she was smiling. "Another good idea is cranberry rows. Uh, do your people use cranberries?"

"Cranberries! Of course. Love 'em," I said. "There's nothing like a good bowl of cranberries. We eat them all the time."

"Right," she said. "Look, Mom went nuts this year and we've got bags of the stuff. I'll drop one off, okay?"

"Super. Thanks, Emily." I hung up. I knew I got the cranberry thing wrong. "Mama!" I yelled. "Mama, we need decorations."

"I know," she grinned coming down the stairs. She was all dressed up. Mama had her church dress on. She was even wearing lipstick. Revlon Fire and Ice. We bought it for the funeral. "No office cleaning today. Go put on your school clothes. We are going to Simpson's right now."

"Simpson's!" I jumped. "Like, to *buy* something?" Sometimes, after we'd finish cleaning Taylor, Laidlaw and Abromovitz, we'd sneak over, but just to look. People like us don't buy things in Simpson's and the salesladies know it. They make me nervous. To be a saleslady at Simpson's they make you dye your hair light blue, and you have to wear glasses that hang down your bosoms on dinky gold chains.

"Yes, to buy something," she laughed. "To buy something and to eat in that big fancy restaurant on the seventh floor."

"Oh my God, the Arcadian Court!" We had their matches of course, but now, now, we were actually going to eat in one of our matchbox restaurants! I was ready in two minutes.

Simpson's is the most elegant place on the planet. This time, Mama and I strolled in like it was all ours. We examined the jewelry counters and considered the makeup. Mama got spritzed by a lady holding Chanel No. 5, and then she spritzed herself with White Shoulders. She looked beautiful in perfume. We browsed through the cocktail dresses and complained about the furniture section. Finally, we sauntered up to the fifth floor to where the Christmas decorations were.

It was magic. There were rows and rows of fake trees decorated every which way. White and pink, blues and reds, and tinsels, and twinkle lights, but the most elegant one was all in gold. "That's it, Mama!" I pointed. "That's class! We'll buy boxes and boxes of nothing but gold decorations." I marched right over to a box of six gold speckled balls. "This one first, okay?"

She smiled and picked up the box.

"Lucija," she hissed, "there must be a mistake. It says $3.79."

"No, not for just one box, Mama." I grabbed other boxes. "Oh no. . . ." I groaned. They all said $3.79! "Look, we really just need the one box. Six balls are plenty, more than enough really. It's far more elegant to have too little. See, it's like when you get all dressed up in your jewelry for the prom. You're supposed to stand in front of the mirror and remove one item of jewelry. We read about that in Carole's *Seventeen* magazine. Carole—"

Mama kissed my head. "It's your Christmas tree, Lucija. You want $3.79 Simpson's balls, you got $3.79 Simpson's balls. Let's go pay and get a hamburger. I'm starving."

The sign at the entrance said: The Hostess Will

Seat You. Please Wait. So we did. There we were in the Arcadian Court. I mean, just like regular Canadians, standing there, waiting for the hostess to seat us. Mama was speechless.

A chandelier the size of a bathtub hung over a shiny black piano was right in the middle of the room. Everything else was in beige and white or white and beige, even the ladies, their clothes, their hair, everything. They all looked like Susan Ambrose's mother. Mama's hair was like the piano, black and shiny. She had on her dark red church coat and I was wearing my green ski jacket. It was practically new. We bought it at Honest Ed's the day I saw Carole. . . . It looked a lot dirtier here than it did at home. My face got hot as the hostess led us to our table. The beige ladies were eyeing us and nudging each other. The hostess gave Mama a gigantic shiny beige menu. Mama pretended to read it and then passed it over to me.

"Oh, oh, Mama," I moaned. "It says: Now Serving Afternoon Tea."

"Such a big menu just to say tea?" said Mama. "No hamburgers?"

"No hamburgers. Just pastries and something called tea sandwiches," I explained. "It's five dollars for two, whichever you choose."

"Okay, the sandwiches," said Mama. "You got to get a lot of sandwiches for five dollars."

A waiter appeared. "Good afternoon, ladies," he sighed. "Tea for two, I presume?"

"Pa sure," beamed Mama in her best English. "Ve like it having dos sandvich vat you gotting 'na menu."

"Perrrrfect," he sighed. "Earl Grey, Darjeeling, Orange Pekoe, Breakfast or Mint?"

"Ya, okay," nodded Mama.

"Uh, Earl Grey, please," I squeaked.

"Perrrrfect." He sighed, scooped up our menus and disappeared.

"I hope that's Salada. Salada tea is the best," said Mama staring after the waiter. "Such a skinny man. Oh! Listen, Lucija. Music!"

She was right. I thought the piano was just for show, but a guy in a black suit had actually started playing it! Neither of us could recognize the song, but it was very pretty. I was so excited. If only the Tomcats could see us now. Lucija Katarina Vukovich having afternoon tea in the Arcadian Court!

The skinny waiter came back with a whole load of stuff. He put down a huge silver teapot, a small silver pot of just hot water, a sugar container and a milk container, two plates you could practically see through, two dinky little cups and saucers, and one teeny tiny plate of sandwiches with no crusts on them.

"Shall I pour?" he sighed.

"No!" scoffed Mama. "I know how is pouring tea. Tank you asking anyvay."

"Perrrrfect," he sighed and vanished.

"You vant it? Now to practicing 'na English?" she asked. The teapot leaked and Mama was drizzling tea all over the place while she pointed to different things. Two beige ladies sitting at the table next to us eyeballed her. "No, no, it's not Friday, after all," I whispered. "Maybe we should stick to Croatian. Quietly."

Mama picked up a crustless wedge. "These are sandwiches?" she laughed. "No wonder he's so skinny. Look, they're green." She bit one. "It's grass. Lucija, they gave us grass sandwiches."

"It's what they call watercress, I think." I sipped my tea. It tasted like flowers.

Mama took a gulp. "This is *not* Salada," she whispered.

The man at the piano finally finished his song. Mama dropped her sandwich and clapped enthusiastically. "Bravo! Bravo!" she called. She was the only one clapping. The piano man looked uncomfortable. The beige ladies were snickering.

"Stop, Mama. Shhh," I hissed. "I am going to die. They're looking at us."

"Don't be such a baby," she laughed. "They are not. Even if they were, who cares? We are here together in this beautiful lovely place enjoying our grass sandwiches."

"Watercress."

"Besides," she leaned over, "we're better than they are. We don't smoke. Look, they're all smoking. Ladies who smoke are *sluts.*" She looked real pleased with herself because she used the English word.

"Not so loud!" I yelled. "That's ridiculous, Mama. What about men who smoke?"

"They're sluts, too," she said.

"Mama," I moaned. "Anyway, I wish Jackie was here."

Mama leaned across the table and patted my hand. "Don't worry about Jackie. Jackie worries about just Jackie."

"Well, I guess so," I said. "Look at the horrible stuff she's gone through, and, well, she's my blood brother, and, I mean, *really,* Mama."

"Jackie," she said, "will always worry about just Jackie."

"That's mean." I finished my sandwich. "Besides, how would you know?"

"I know," she smiled. "I see when you're all together."

It was hopeless. She just point blank doesn't understand about things. I was still hungry. "Five dollars just for this, Mama. I'm sorry."

"No, no, no, Lucija. It's *perrrr*fect," she beamed. "They have to pay the man on the piano, all these skinny waiters, plus the lady who sits you down. It's a deal. I love it. Now, let's go back to our Onlyhouse and decorate your tree. Christmas is waiting for us."

We tipped the waiter, shook hands with the piano player and congratulated the hostess for working in such a pretty place. I sang Christmas songs in the subway. I know I was supposed to be sad. Carole was dead and everything. I kept reminding myself about the funeral, the coffin and stuff . . . but . . . *my* house . . . *my* Christmas tree. I looked at Mama sitting in her church coat and lipstick. She looked stunning.

Chapter Ten

"**S**o eat your sandwich," I said. "It's got real Miracle Whip on it."

Jackie was at my house for lunch. It was a Friday, two months after Christmas, but it was one of those days off public schools get all the time. I had all the special food I had seen at her house: cheese slices in plastic wrapping, white bread and Miracle Whip salad dressing. She wasn't eating.

"Yeah." She took a bite and stared out the kitchen window.

"You okay?" I asked.

"Yeah," she sighed. "No. It's her. . . . February twenty-second. It would've been her birthday today. She's—she would have been seventeen."

"Oh," I said.

"I'm not hungry, I guess."

"Well," I grabbed her sandwich. "Want to do something about it?"

"I am not going to light any stupid candles!" she said. "So if you're going to, go on."

"No, I've got that covered. I've been lighting candles for Carole's soul since before Christmas, and I'm going to keep at it until Easter. But that's not it. I mean, do you want to do something about her birthday?"

"Yeah, right," she snorted. "Like what, bake a cake?"

"Like send her a card," I said.

"Unbelievable. Do these things just come to you or what?" She shook her head.

"No, I mean it!" I said. "Look, I don't even know when my dad's birthday is, but Father's Day used to be real bad. It's such a big deal at school, right? You gotta make a special card and stuff. Every year, I'd have to remind the Sister about him being dead and everything, and every year the Sisters would feel all sorry for me. Then they'd make the class count their blessings and say a prayer for the departed."

"So!" she said.

"So . . ." I gulped. "So when we moved to Hakim's, and I went over to St. Therese's, I stopped reminding the Sisters. I'd make the most beautiful fabulous card in the class. Right after school, I'd go straight to the cemetery and wish him a happy Father's Day. Then I'd bury the card."

"You're a mental case, Lucy," she said.

"No! Listen!" I said. "It stopped everyone feeling sorry for me, and I, well, it feels right. I kinda tell him things and . . . and . . . I'm pretty sure he likes the cards."

She wrinkled her nose. "Hmmm. I dunno. . . . Well, maybe. All right, okay! Let's do it!"

"Now?" I asked. "We're supposed to meet everyone for garage roof racing."

"Not for another couple of hours," she said. "Where's that construction paper I hauled?"

"There's just a couple of sheets left; see, the Christmas tree took up—"

"I just need the one," she said, "and a pencil."

I rounded everything up. She slapped a green

sheet together and scribbled Happy Birthday Carole on the outside and Love Jackie on the inside. That was it. Nothing else.

"Let's go," she said.

I used to spend hours doing my dad's card.

While we were walking over to the Mount Pleasant Cemetery, Jackie wanted to know when my father had died.

"When I was a baby, like I said."

"No, when exactly?"

I remembered the crumpled yellow scrap of paper. "April 16, 1957. Why?"

"No reason," she shrugged. "Look, there's the Ghost." We were walking along Bayview near Moore Avenue, and she was pointing to a white building across from Loblaws.

"They went there a lot, Carole and a bunch of Rosedale jerks."

"It's empty," I said. "Why would they go there?"

She shrugged.

Finally we got to *Here Lies Carole Patricia Lewis, Beloved Daughter* . . . etcetera. Jackie turned to me. "So now what?"

"Now we dig," I said. There was hardly any snow, but the ground was frozen solid. We scraped and heaved and kicked. It was no use. We finally settled on shoving the card between the headstone and this dead little bush. I swore it would be just as good.

"So?" she said. "That's it?"

"Well, I dunno exactly," I said. It was a dark and dirty day, just like at the funeral. We were the only ones there. "Want to sing 'Happy Birthday'?"

"Jeez Louise! You are nuts." Then she kicked the headstone. Right on the *Beloved* part. "They all take off, you know. They just up and take off."

I stared at *Here Lies Carole* . . .

"I yelled at her that day," she said. "I yelled at her for skipping school, and I said I wouldn't cover her fat ass anymore. . . . Jeez. . . . Jeez."

"I won't, Jackie. I won't take off on you."

"No," she wiped her face with her ski jacket. "No, you won't, Lucy." She threw her arm around me and started to giggle. "You won't go because you need me, and you're too smart to forget it."

My stomach disintegrated.

"No–o–o–o!" I wanted to smack her. "Why would you—how could—"

"Forget it. Let's go," she shrugged. "We're late."

I fumed all the way back to the laneway. How could she say that?

Cindy and Jenny were there, ready to go. "Where were you guys?" called Jenny.

"Business," snapped Jackie. "Okay, Lucy and me in the first heat. You and Cindy in the next one. Winner takes all in the third heat. Come on. Come on."

We ran to the Cleveland Street end of the laneway. Everyone loved garage roof racing. It was Jackie's idea. Jackie had a million great ideas, but garage roof racing was the best. We started just after Christmas when it was really icy. She had been perfecting it since.

Two of us would get into starting positions at the Cleveland Street end, and the other two would spot a runner. You know, running alongside, screaming at them to hurry. You had to climb up the first backyard fence, then tightrope walk to the first garage. Then you go up, over and down to the next fence and on until you got to the Bayview end. If you hit the ground, you're disqualified. It was brilliant.

When Jackie was in a really good mood, she'd let Susan Ambrose and Lisa Kirkland join in. They're like alternate members of the Tomcats. Well, more like go-fers-in-waiting, but they weren't there today.

There's nothing like it, nothing. You can hear the blood pumping in your head and you're scared out of your mind, but when you hit those roofs just right, you fly.

"Okay," called Jackie. "I had the right side last time, so we'll switch."

"On your marks!" screamed Cindy.

We started just like in the Olympics. One knee down.

"Get ready."

Our bums went up.

"Get set."

I was a rocket waiting for takeoff.

"Go!"

I scrambled up the fence and tightroped the ledge until I got to my first roof. Jackie was already over her first peak. I roared up and slid down, not enough time for the fence.

I'd have to jump to the next roof—but the snow! I made it, but I hit my knee. Clutching the shingles, I crawled up the peak. The next backyard didn't have a garage. I tightroped along two sets of fences. Then there was the Miller's flat garage and a big leap to the Stablers' old one. She was still ahead. I raced along the next fence, my chest burning. My knee was sore. It was great! We were neck and neck, but there was too much of a gap for another jump. I tightroped the Anderson fence and roared over our clubhouse roof.

She was behind, but just.

I shut my eyes and threw myself onto the Peterson garage. Over, then down, I heaved myself onto the last peak and rolled onto the ground. Jackie jumped.

"Tie," she yelled.

"No way!" I screamed.

"Tie!" she glared.

"I hit the ground first!"

"It's not who hits the ground; it's who hits the last roof!" she said. "I made up the rules, remember? Right, guys?"

"Yeah," mumbled Jenny. We all shuffled back to the Cleveland Street end again.

"Great race, Lucy," Jackie grinned. "You wanna start this one?"

"Yeah, sure," I said. "On your marks!" We practically always tied. "Get ready!" I did hit the ground first. "Get set." Well, it was her game. "Go!"

I was spotting Cindy. It was snowing hard. "Be careful!" She slipped badly on the second roof. Jenny was ahead.

"Faster," I yelled. "She's way ahead."

Cindy jumped. There was a horrible scream. Jenny jumped off. Jackie raced toward me. "Cindy!" I was stuck in slow motion. Everybody was stuck in slow motion.

"Is she dead?" called Jenny.

"Ow, ow, ow." Cindy lay in a heap on the Stablers' woodpile. "My arm," she whimpered.

"Shit," said Jackie.

We squeezed around the woodpile and got her to sit up. Dirty tears streamed down her face.

"I . . . I think it's broken." She was chewing her lip.

"Shit," said Jackie.

"What do we do?" wailed Jenny. "We've got to get her home."

"Don't be a jerk," said Jackie. "We'll get brained."

"My mom's not home." Cindy was shaking.

"We've got to go to a hospital," I said.

"What's the matter with you guys?" barked Jackie.

73

"If anyone finds out what we were doing, we're dead. Dead, dead, dead. We'll fix it."

"We've just got to go to a hospital," I repeated. "Does anyone know where Sick Kids is?"

They shook their heads. "Downtown somewhere?" said Jenny.

I couldn't think. "Uh, so we'll go to Sunnybrook Veteran's Hospital. That's it. The Davisville bus goes right in there. How much money do we got?"

"You gotta be in the army," said Jackie.

"My dad was in the army," said Jenny, "but he's retired."

"Perfect," I said, "that makes him a veteran."

"You can't go to a hospital!" yelled Jackie. "I've, uh, got to go home to, uh, baby-sit and you screwups are gonna screw up without me there!"

Cindy threw up on the woodpile.

"I thought your mom was home today," said Jenny.

"Since when do you know anything, turnip head?" Jackie turned to me. "Here's thirty cents. It's all I got. Get a story and stick to it, for Chrissake. I've got to go."

She left. She actually left.

Jenny and Cindy looked at me as if I knew what to do.

"Well?" asked Jenny.

"Well," I shrugged. "Well, let's get her up. We're going to Sunnybrook."

We heaved Cindy up and almost broke her other arm. "Ow, ow, ow," she moaned.

"She needs a sling or something," said Jenny.

"Good idea." I took off my ski jacket, put her arm in the hood and tied the jacket arms around her neck. She looked like a goof, but at least she was standing.

We stumbled to the Davisville bus stop. I was shivering and they were both crying. When the bus turned up, I got on first.

"Hi there," I smiled at the driver. "Uh, see, the three of us have to go to Sunnybrook because one of us has broken her arm. However, we seem to be exactly twelve cents short."

"Kids. Get on. Get on." He didn't take our money.

We sat on that long bench behind the driver propping up Cindy between us. She was great. She never stopped crying, but she was real quiet about it.

"My mom's gonna barbecue me," she hiccuped.

"Don't think about it," I ordered. "See what happened is . . . we were just walking along . . ."

"Yeah, yeah," they nodded.

"Minding our own business . . ." I stopped.

"Yeah, yeah," they urged.

"When a little kid on a tricycle comes whipping by, and Cindy falls over trying to get out of his way and breaks her—"

"A hit-and-run tricycle?" asked Jenny.

"Okay, okay," I said. "A really big kid on a really big racing bike and he doesn't stop either. Good, huh?"

"Good, uh-huh, good." They nodded.

"Okay, kids," called the driver. "We're here. See those double glass doors? You go through there; that's Emergency. Then you turn left and go to the first desk you see."

"Thanks, Mister," I called.

We shuffled single file through these really tricky automatic doors. The waiting area was empty except for two little old ladies sitting at opposite ends of the room.

"You talk," hissed Jenny when we got to the desk.

"Good afternoon," I said, a little too loud. "Her father," I pointed to Jenny, "was in the army. Is that okay?"

"Name?"

"Uh, well. Mine, the army dad's or Cindy's?" I asked.

"Patient's name?"

"Well, the one with the broken arm is Cindy, Cindy Spencer. See, this kid on a tricycle."

"Date of Birth?"

"I, uh, dunno." I turned to Cindy.

"Thirteen October 1955," she said. "Not a tricycle."

"That's right," I said. "Not a tricycle. A really big racer, a really big kid—"

"OHIP?"

"And he didn't even . . . what's an OHIP?" I asked.

"Her health insurance number." She was typing all this down.

"Uh oh," moaned Jenny.

I leaned over the counter and peered at her name tag. "Uh, you see, Miss Mulhullen, in the confusion . . . we must have neglected to bring the number. How about, you stick a cast on her right now, and then we'll go straight home and mail you the number? We don't want to go and upset a whole bunch of people." I winked at her.

Miss Mulhullen stopped typing. "Look, honey," she sighed, "I can see you're in a bind. But I need names. I need addresses. I need lots of numbers and I need parents."

"I can't remember my dad's work number," wailed Cindy, "and my mom's shopping."

Miss Mulhullen ignored her. "So we'll have to call

somebody's dad, and somebody's dad has got to turn up here with her dad." She was pounding on the counter.

"Well, that lets me out." I turned to Jenny. She was the only one with a dad that was home all the time.

"My dad was in the army, sure," stammered Jenny, "but he never went overseas or nothing. Is that okay?"

Miss Mulhullen rolled her eyes. "This is not *just* a veteran's hospital, kid. Dr. Peters . . ." She flagged down someone who looked like a teenager in a white coat. "We're getting the parents; it's the right arm." He disappeared with Cindy.

Miss Mulhullen zeroed in on Jenny. "Everybody's name, your phone number and your father's full name, now!" Jenny dribbled out the details. "Fine," she glared at us. "I will arrange for Mr. Clarke to contact the rest of your parents. Now, go sit down and behave yourselves."

"Jeez, you'd think an army nurse would be friendlier," said Jenny.

We crawled to the waiting room. For the next half hour, I shivered and Jenny sobbed. "Stop that!" I hissed. "We'll be fine. Just stick to the story. Got it?"

"Got it," she sniffled.

"Sure?" I said.

"Sure, I'm sure," she whined.

Just then Mr. Clarke stormed through the automatic doors. He was purple. Mr. Clarke was followed by Mr. Spencer and, oh God, Mama. While he was still stomping over, Jenny jumped right up and committed suicide. "A really big tricycle whipped by while we were garage roof racing and Cindy fell onto the Slater woodpile and we'll never ever do it again!"

What a mess.

When all the yelling stopped and the OHIP numbers got sorted out, well . . . we were grounded until Easter. That was more than a month away. Mr. Clarke was personally going to call Mrs. Lewis. God.

Finally, at 7:45 p.m., Cindy came bopping out. She had on a great big grin and a truly superior white cast. Absolutely nobody smiled back. We filed out in deadly silence and got into Mr. Clarke's car. It was like being under water.

When we got to our Onlyhouse Mama straightened up. "I be tanking you, Meester Clarke." She practically pushed me out of the car.

"Careful, Mama. See, my knee really hurts." That was usually good for a big response.

Nothing.

We walked ever so slowly up the path. I was dragging my leg and wincing.

Nothing.

At the top of the stairs, Mama stopped and examined the porch light. I decided not to breathe.

"So," she said, "who won?"

"I did, Mama!" I burst. "She tried to make it a tie, but I won, really."

She shook her head and put her key in the lock.

"Good," she said.

Chapter Eleven

*E*ver since the funeral, Jackie always wore lipstick. Sandpebble Beige by Bonnie Bell. It's what Carole always wore. It didn't look right on Jackie. It looked goofy or spooky, but not right.

Anyway, we were all just sitting around on our garbage cans. The clubhouse was dark plus it reeked of cat pee and wet dirt. It was nice outside. No flowers yet, but little green shoots were popping up all over the place. Emily McDonald had joined a girls' three pitch team. Jackie said that three pitch was for sucky Girl Guide types.

I'd like to try three pitch sometime.

We were having a seance. We had seances all the time, ever since garage roof racing was out. Sometimes we frigged around with Carole's old Ouija Board. I was at Jackie's when Mrs. Lewis found it under Jackie's bed and threw it in the garbage, complaining about it being evil and dirty. I helped Jackie sneak it out of the bin and over to the clubhouse. Cindy's cast had finally came off four days ago and her arm was really gross. It was all white and cheesy looking. Even Jackie was impressed.

Sometimes we scared each other stupid—with the Ouija Board, I mean—but we never actually got a real live dead person. It's a weird thing about scaring yourself. If it goes perfect, it's like your heart is pumping in your teeth, you're going to explode and then, it's all okay. You want to lie down. It's over.

Jenny always put on the crucifix Mama made me wear, and I had to bring in my rosary for Cindy. They both promised to turn Catholic when they grew up. Jackie didn't believe in anybody's God, just dead people.

So we were just hanging around, but you could tell Jackie was bored. You could mainly tell because she was destroying Jenny again. I'll never figure out why Jenny took it. Jackie would say something seriously mean, and Jenny would just sit there like a tree stump and nod. This was like spraying gasoline on a fire.

"Quit grinning at me, you pukey little toad!" she roared.

"Oh, let's not start this again," I said. "It's so boring."

"Well, excu–u–u–se me!" sneered Jackie. "We can't bore our Iroquois royalty."

"That was my grandmother."

"Ha!" she said. "You left out a couple of great greats didn't you, princess? Anyway you're right. I've been thinking—we need some real Tomcat excitement. I have an absolutely stupendous idea. Any decent sort of club needs a uniform, right?" We nodded. She fished around in her pocket. "Well, the official Tomcat uniform will be . . . Sandpebble Beige lipstick by Bonnie Bell."

"Oh great," I thought. For Mama, kids who wore lipstick were right up there with ladies who smoked.

"You mean we gotta buy a lipstick?" whined Jenny.

"No, candy ass," said Jackie. "You steal it from Cheevers' just like I did."

I was stunned. What next? Now I had to steal something? Aside from maybe being thrown in jail, aside from maybe burning in Hell or at least Purgatory for a while, stealing was one of those knives-in-Jesus's-heart type of things. Sister Magdalene was deadly serious about that. Maybe God doesn't fuss much about what Protestants do or don't do. Like, they don't have to make a sign of the cross when they hear an ambulance siren. But stealing? Nobody's religion says, "Go forth and steal something."

"Great idea," I said. "Who's first?"

"Way to go, Lucy," she grinned. "I figure turnip head goes tomorrow. Then if she doesn't run right home and tell her daddy all about it, Cindy can go on Wednesday. On Saturday you go, okay? You can make one Saturday, eh?"

Saturday? Saturday I cleaned offices with Mama. They didn't know about that, of course. For all these months, they thought I spent the whole day shopping in the Jewish market. "Sure. Super," I said. "Super plan."

The next day at 4:45 p.m., Jenny charged into the clubhouse. *Ta da!* She flashed a Sandpebble Beige lipstick. Just like that. It was amazing. I don't know. I guess, I thought you should look different after you stole something.

"Good stuff, reject," said Jackie.

"Was it tough?" asked Cindy. "Mrs. Cheevers is such a witch. She won't even sell candy just to keep kids out of her store."

"Hell, no!" bragged Jenny. "You can hear the old bat coming from one end of the store to the other."

Mrs. Cheevers ran Cheevers' Druggists and Sundries by herself. No one, not even the parents, could remember a Mr. Cheevers. Mrs. Cheevers smoked

Players unfiltered cigarettes, and she always had two going. One was lit by the cash register and one was stuck to the gobs of orange lipstick plastered on her mouth.

"No sweat, allouette," said Jenny. "A baby could do it."

On Wednesday, Cindy stumbled in looking barf green.

"So any problems?" asked Jackie.

"No, no, well, no," whispered Cindy. "I got it, see." She started smearing on the lipstick. "Does it look okay?"

Now Cindy looked like what someone who had stolen something was supposed to look like.

"It looks cool," said Jackie. "Okay, let's have a quick seance, and then we'll meet here on Saturday at two o'clock. By then Lucy will have her lipstick. I'm telling you, guys, the whole world is gonna see us coming and get out of our way."

"Can't wait," I said.

That night, I told Mama that Mrs. Lewis had a major crisis at the Silver Rail Tavern and that I had promised to help Jackie baby-sit Karen and Kyle on Saturday. "Jackie again," she said.

"Well, I've got to. You know how I worry about her."

"Lucija." She paused. "It's a good thing to worry about people. It's a good thing to help, *but*—"

"She's my blood brother!" I threw up my hands.

"Lucija, where was your *blood brother* when you needed her at the hospital?"

My face burned. "Jackie has responsibilities," I said.

Mama examined the ceiling. "Go. Go and have fun."

On Saturday morning, I got out a pencil and

examined my personal list of Sins Versus Indulgences. Regular sinning gets you into Purgatory. Indulgences get you out. Sister Magdalene explained the whole system in grade three. I've been fine-tuning it ever since.

An Indulgence doesn't pay for your sins like confession or penance, although you've got to keep up with it if you're going to do any sinning. See, pretty well everybody has to do time in Purgatory before they go to Heaven. It's not a great place, but it's a lot better than Hell. An Indulgence means you get so much time off your stay in Purgatory for doing certain things. In the old days you could just pay off a priest or build a church and go straight to Heaven. One of the popes changed the rules because Heaven was getting too crowded with rich people.

Anyway, it's like you get fifty days off for going to Mass during a weekday and a hundred for wearing a scapular medal. That's a necklace with a picture of a major approved holy person on it. Stuff like that. When I was nine, I figured it all out mathematically. My system doesn't get you out of Hell though. Once you're in Hell, you're there for life. It's a great system. I even convinced Shernee Chandaria that it would work for Hindu people.

I hauled Shernee to Mass every single morning, seven days a week, for a month. Her mom thought we were nuts. We said the rosary endlessly. We wore eleven scapular medals all the time, even in the bath. We rescued birds that didn't need rescuing and dragged a thousand little Italian ladies across Bathurst at College. I figured I could take the Lord's name in vain a whole bunch of times, covet my neighbor's wife plus lie a lot and still go straight to Heaven. Steal a lipstick? No problem.

Cheevers' Druggists and Sundries was dark, and

smoky of course. I tripped into the store. She wheezed at me right off. "Whadda ya want, kid?"

"Uh, just looking at the, uh, your . . . sundries." I gave her my nearly best smile.

"Looking ain't free in here. You gotta—" She was interrupted by a coughing attack. "You gotta buy something."

Mrs. Cheevers was really something. It wasn't that she was fat so much as just really loose, all over. Every time she said something her jowls shook and her chins quivered. The most amazing thing was her hair. She didn't have much, but every little yellow strand was always wrapped into tight little curls held together by black bobby pins. The bobby pins made an *X* over every single curl. It was like her whole head was one big mistake.

"Sure," I grinned. "I am planning to buy at least one sundry."

I slunk past the card section over to the makeup section. Maybeline, Yardley, Revlon, Cover-Girl— where was it? A-ha, Bonnie Bell! I listened for Mrs. Cheevers. . . . Nothing. Deep breath. I started to reach, but that picture of the sad Jesus with his heart all covered in thorns kept getting in the way of the lipstick. I shut my eyes and grabbed!

Well, it didn't burn or anything. Easy, no big deal. *Thief, robber!* I stuck it in my pocket and inched toward the door. *Robber! Thief!* Cover-Girl, Revlon, Yardley, Maybeline, the card section—almost there. Did I look different? *Thief! Thief!*

"So whadda ya wanna buy, kid?" she rasped.

My feet disappeared into the floor. "The lipstick," I croaked.

"What lipstick?" Her eyes narrowed.

I fumbled in my pocket. "This one. It's for my mom."

"I'm having a real run on that shade lately." She started hacking again. "Eighty-two cents with tax."

Eighty-two cents! Perfect. Well, my life was over. "I've only got seventy-five." I shook all the way back to the makeup section. I was at Maybeline when she yelled.

"Okay, kid, seventy-five, but keep your trap shut." Unbelievable! You couldn't do better at the Jewish market. I ran back. "Thanks a million," I said, dumping my three quarters on the counter. I tore out and didn't stop until I got to the clubhouse. There they were, huddled over the Ouija Board.

"I did it!" I screamed.

"Yeah? Good," shrugged Jackie. "Sit down. Sit down. We've been talking. I have another absolutely stupendous idea!"

Wait a minute!. Hey, where was my "Way to go, Lucy. Good work" or "Great stuff"? I mean, I did practically, almost steal something. I sat down and very loudly did not put on my lipstick. "Okay, okay. Now what?"

"Well," began Cindy, "do you think you could wake yourself up before midnight? Say by 11:30 or so?"

"Yeah," I said. "I get up every night at 11:00 o'clock, no matter what."

"What for?" asked Jenny.

"I get up to check if Mama's still breathing," I said.

"Ha!" barked Jackie. "Now I've heard everything."

"It's not funny," I yelled. "It's not! Mama's mama, my Baka, died in her sleep when she was forty-one! It was during the war. One day the Nazis killed two of my uncles. That night, while Mama was sleeping with her, Baka's heart just stopped and she died. That sort of thing gets passed down you know. Mama's forty-four. I've been watching her for three years now."

"That makes sense," nodded Cindy.

"Yeah, so," I calmed down. "It's just me and Mama, you know. If she died, I'd be an orphan. I'd have to make plans and everything before the government found her. They'd ship me back to Zagreb. I think I've got an aunt there. Nobody's shipping me back. I'm Canadian, you know. I've got papers and everything."

"Of course you are," said Jenny. "You don't even have an accent."

"You could live with me," offered Cindy.

"That's stupendous!" said Jackie. "You're just full of dead people! We're bound to get someone with you at the Ghost.

"The Bayview Ghost?" I choked. "That deserted building?"

"Yeah, yeah, that's the plan!" said Jackie. "Look, we're not getting anyone here because no one's croaked in this garage. So we're going to have a seance at midnight at the Bayview Ghost. You know the real reason they didn't finish the building is because that whole field has always been haunted."

"Yeah!" interrupted Jenny. "It happened before you got here. While they were putting it up, there were a lot of weird accidents—twilight zone type of stuff. Finally, when they got to the roof, one of the guys fell off and broke his neck in two thousand pieces."

"But that's not all," Jackie glared at her. "One week later a construction guy went berserk and murdered the foreman with a power drill. Isn't that great? Anyway, all the workers refused to come back. The developer went bankrupt or killed himself or something."

"You *know*," said Cindy, "my dad says tramps sleep in there and the police always come around to chase them out."

"Tough nuts," said Jackie. "We can outrun a few winos and some fat cops. Fart-face will bring a flashlight. I'm bringing candles, and Cindy's going to bring the Ouija Board. All you have to do is bring that cross you always wear. Just in case you need it."

I was trapped. They had it all planned out. "I don't know. This is serious. We're doing so much stuff, you know. Couldn't we just hang out or—what *is* it with you and dead people?"

Jackie stood up. Her face was in mine. "You loved all of it," she smiled. "Don't you get it, Lucy? If we bring someone back, we'll be famous, superstars. Everyone will know who we are. We'll all be Somebody!"

"Yeah, Somebody!" said Jenny.

"I'd sure like to be Somebody," said Cindy.

It was all upside down. God, it was like going backward on the ferris wheel! They were so incredibly popular—popular and perfectly Canadian. Blue eyes, blonde hair, beige mothers, the whole bit. All this time, from September to April, I had done every single little thing to be exactly like them. I mean, I got to go to a whole bunch of parties this year just because I hung out with them. If they weren't Somebody, who were they?

"Okay," I shrugged, "I guess I want to be Somebody, too."

"Great!" said Jackie, staring at me. "We'd hate to lose you on the brink of stardom, eh, guys? Hey, didn't your dad die around now?"

"I told you already, on April sixteenth. It'll be ten years; he died ten years ago." God.

"Perfect, that's too perfect!" She kept staring at me. "That's next Friday! A lining up of death anniversaries is good. So we'll all sneak out and meet then, at 11:30 sharp, at the bottom of Cleveland and Merton."

They all began to buzz and put finishing touches to The Plan. I felt sick. "Right," I mumbled. "I've gotta go. See you guys at school."

What a mess, what a mess. What if my dad saw me? I know he watches me. God, setting fires, stealing, sneaking out . . . I hoped he was busy. Not only that, but they hardly noticed when I did all that stuff. Yeah. "Well, I'll show them," I spit. "I'm never ever going to wear that stupid lipstick."

Chapter Twelve

"*W*ell, don't you think she's gorgeous?" I asked in English. It was an English-only day. Mama and I were talking about Jackie. So maybe I talked about her a lot. "I think she's gorgeous; course not as gorgeous as Carole was gorgeous, but she is gorgeous, huh?"

"Too skinny, too yellow," said Mama between sips of coffee.

"*Blonde*, Mama," I said. "The word is *blonde.*"

It was Friday, *the* Friday, and we were having Friday coffee. It's the sort of thing we always did—Mama would get out a beautiful little copper carafe and boil up some Turkish coffee.

Turkish coffee looks and tastes like black paint. Mama loved it. I had this beautiful big cup that looked like a bowl with a handle. Mama would put in about a tablespoon of the coffee, some sugar, and fill it up to the brim with hot frothy milk. It was better than magic.

"Okay, okay, again, so you be reminding me again vy she be too *perrrr*fect."

Ever since our lunch in the Arcadian Court, *perrrr-fect* was Mama's favorite English word.

"You know, she's, oh . . ." I sighed. "Well, just everyone at Maurice Cody looks up to Jackie. She's got guts and she makes things happen. Jackie is a Somebody, Mama, and when I'm with her, I'm Somebody, too."

"Lucija." She got up and gave me one of those killer hugs where you can't breathe. "You most big Somebody 'na whole school. 'Na whole world!"

"Mama," I mumbled into her blouse, "let go. You're just pretending not to understand. Jackie is cool. Even the teachers leave her alone. And I bet her family came here like a thousand years ago.

"So!" she smiled. "They coming 'na boat, too!"

"Mama, I want to be just like Jackie. I pray and pray to be exactly like her."

"Lucija," Mama shook her head, "you be tanking God vun day to not listening dose praying."

"Right!" I rolled my eyes. "Like you're going to spend a whole lot of time and effort praying for something, then be real grateful when it doesn't happen. Really, Mama!"

"You be seeing," she laughed. It drove me crazy when she got like that. Like she knew something I didn't, but she wasn't going to tell me what. We finished our coffee and went out to work on the garden. No vegetables for our Onlyhouse. No sir. I was planning a real English-type garden with tons and tons of ivy and roses. We could only afford one rosebush so far, but it looked real English.

It was after nine by the time I had my bath. When I came down I found Mama fast asleep in front of her sewing at the kitchen table. She did that a lot. Sometimes it made me angry, but I never knew at who. I touched her shoulder. "Come on, Mama. That's enough for now. It's our bedtime."

For two hours, I lay there waiting and gulping air. 11:07, 11:13, 11:15, it was time. I was afraid to get up.

I could pretend I slept through. No. I slid out of bed and crept over to the dirty laundry. After I put on what I had worn that day, I tiptoed over to Mama. Still breathing. I made two signs of the cross and left.

I stood outside on the verandah and breathed in the night. 11:30 p.m. smelled a lot different from 11:30 a.m. It sounded different, too. A car three blocks away sounded like it was going to run over your feet. And it was seriously dark. 11:30 p.m. is a lot darker than, say, 9:30 p.m. I'd been out at 9:30 p.m. lots of times. I didn't want to go. I really didn't want to go. My heart was in my teeth again. God, I felt so bad that it felt so good. After double-checking the street, I bolted down Cleveland, over to Merton and right up to Bayview. Jackie was standing under a street lamp.

"Hi, Lucy," she grinned. "Any problems?"

"Huh?" I said.

"I said hi," she said. "You okay?"

"I can't hear," I whispered. "My heart's too loud. There's just boom, boom, boom."

"Relax," she smiled, "I'm here. We're together. I told you nothing can touch us when we're together. That's why we're blood brothers."

"Huh?"

"Yup," she nodded. "Remember on that first day when Gladbags singled you out and went on and on about you? What a browner you were."

"Don't remind me," I said.

"Well, first you looked like you were gonna drop dead and sob your guts out, but then you just marched back to your desk like it all happened to someone else. I knew you had the stuff."

"So why'd you try to beat me up?"

"Had to be sure," she shrugged. Just then we heard a sound like the distant rumbling of elephants.

Jenny and Cindy were bopping in and out of parked cars giggling their heads off.

"Keep it down!" yelled Jackie. "You sound like an earthquake."

"Sorry, sorry."

"Okay," she said. "Ouija Board?"

"Check," said Cindy.

"Flashlight?"

"Check," said Jenny.

"Crucifix?"

"Check," I said.

"And I've got the candles and matches," said Jackie. "Okay, Tomcats, let's get famous!"

"Wait!" said Jenny, turning to me. "Didn't you bring your rosary thing? You always bring your rosary thing."

"No one said to bring it."

"I don't want to get dead people without the rosary thing," she whined.

"Stop being such a suck," snapped Jackie. "She's got the stupid crucifix. That'll do. Now let's go. Quietly."

Jenny started to shiver. So did I. 11:30 p.m. is cold.

We skulked onto Bayview, trotted single file across Moore Avenue and slithered down the Extension and across Nesbitt Street. At the bottom of the field, Jackie stopped. We all crashed into each other.

"Ow!" said Cindy.

"Watch it!" yelled Jackie.

"Wow!" whispered Jenny.

There it was, hulking above us in the moonlight. A deserted corpse of a building surrounded by a black empty field. The building was made out of a pale shiny brick. It glowed like white neon. The Ghost was six stories high, and there were large gaping pits of black where the windows should've been. Dark rust marks drizzled down the sides from the roof. It was wounded and bleeding.

"Right," Jackie gulped. "At the back right corner, some of the boards are off one of the doors. We can crawl through there."

The field oozed mud. It oozed and vibrated. My legs buzzed with every single step. Nobody else seemed to notice. The Ghost was singing to me . . . or warning me. We got to the door.

"Okay, runt, you first," said Jackie.

"Why me?" cried Jenny.

"You've got the flashlight, dope!" she said.

"Well, maybe, if we—" began Cindy.

"I'll go, I'll go," I said, grabbing the flashlight. I climbed in and blinked through the dust and filth. It tasted bad. Even with the flashlight, you couldn't see the walls. It was like you knew you were inside, but inside of what? What was I doing here? "It's okay," I coughed. "Just be careful. It's an awful mess."

Jackie crawled in, Cindy next, then Jenny. There were boards and bricks, cement blocks and broken beer bottles everywhere. "We have a lot of tidying to do," said Cindy.

"We're having a seance, not a tea party," said Jackie. "We'll have to move some stuff around though. Put that board over those bricks and get some blocks for chairs."

"It's too cold in here," said Jenny. "Why is it so cold in here? It's not this cold outside."

"Shut up and clean," said Jackie.

"Eaggghhh!"

"Cindy!" we all screamed.

"Cindeeeeeee!"

"It's okay. I just tripped over a block. I thought it was a body," she giggled.

"Spare me," muttered Jackie.

When we were almost ready, I heard Jenny whimpering behind me.

"No, no, no."

"What?" I shuffled over. "What is it?"

"I'm going to die," she was sniffling.

"Are you crying?" I whispered.

"I think I peed my pants."

"Already?" I said. "We haven't done anything yet!"

"I'm dead," she gulped. "Jackie is going to destroy me. You know she'll destroy me. Piece by piece."

"She's not going to destroy anyone. I promise," I said under my breath. "Look, she won't know. Make sure you sit beside me." She was still crying. "Here, you wear my crucifix, okay? I've got leftover protection from having communion on Sunday."

"You're a real pal, Lucy," she sniffled.

"Let's go, you guys," called Jackie. "Little Suzy Homemaker here has finished tidying." Jenny and I picked our way over the garbage.

Cindy had set up the Ouija Board over two cement blocks. Jackie lit three candles and stuck them into empty beer bottles. I looked at Cindy and Jackie, and I looked at Jenny. I could barely recognize them. I wonder if I would have been able to recognize myself.

"Who are we gonna get?" asked Jenny.

"What about Lucy's dad?" suggested Cindy.

"Right," I said. "Like I want him to know that I've just snuck out of the house at midnight. What if we can't send him back? What if he decides to march right over and tell Mama?"

"Oh yeah," giggled Cindy. "But I don't know any dead people except old Mr. McGyver around the corner. He doesn't count, does he? How about you, Jenny?"

"Well," she said, "I think I have a dead grandfather, but I never knew him. What would we talk about? Apparently, nobody got along."

"Never mind," said Jackie. "We're going to get Carole."

We all stopped breathing.

"Oh–h–h–h, I don't know, Jackie." I shook my head. "You see, because of the way she, uh, passed on, she could be in a sort of in-between type of place, hanging around with in-between type of people. You can't guarantee that they won't come with her, you know."

"I don't care!" she said. "She came here all the time with the jerk. See, we'll get her here; she knows to come to the Ghost. I gotta talk to Carole and I'm going to talk to Carole."

My stomach tangled and then snapped in two. All these months I had prayed over Carole's soul in Purgatory. What if I got that wrong? What if she was burning right now? You don't call up people frying in Hell.

"No, think about it, Jackie," I said. "It won't work. All that stuff with Carole and you, it didn't matter. She did it because . . . because . . . I don't know, but you couldn't fix her then and you can't fix her now."

She looked right through me. "I have to talk to her and you know why. She liked you, Lucy. She thought you were so neat. I finally found a good friend, she said. I am going to talk to her and you have to help. I have to say sorry. Lucy, she'd want you to help."

There, that's it. She was doing it again, twisting me. I don't like being twisted.

"Okay, guys?" she asked.

We nodded grimly and started up our routine.

95

Everyone put their index and middle fingers on the wedge. "Omm, omm, omm." I don't know why we *omm*ed, but we *omm*ed. I always thought it had something to do with Buddha. "Omm, omm, omm."

"Spirits, spirits, are you near? Spirits, spirits, are you here?"

The wedge took off! Jackie gasped. It slid smoothly to the right. Straight to the *Yes* symbol. It had never gone there before.

"Oh God!" shuddered Jenny.

"Shhh!" We all shushed.

"Keep going," Jackie's voice broke. "Spirits, spirits, do you have my big sis—I mean do you have Carole Patricia Lewis with you?"

The wedge jerked and swung fast back to the YES. Whoa! I knew for sure I wasn't pushing that thing. Time to stop.

"Spirits, spirits, is Carole in Heaven?"

My hand was yanked over to the *No* symbol. NO? Oh Jesus. No!

"Spirits, sprits." Jackie stopped. "Spirits, may we speak to her?" There was a smell, a new smell, a rotting smell. We heard rumbling. The wedge swung violently to *Yes* again. Yes!

"No!" cried Jenny. "I don't want to!"

Jackie stood up and glared at Jenny. "Shut up, turd!" An icy gust of wind sputtered in, boards rattled and two of the candles blew out. There was a roar. Somebody screamed. Lights hit the building. A car door slammed, then another. A faint voice crackled. "Affirmative, fifty-three." Another voice: "Try the windows."

"Get out!" screamed Jackie. "It's the cops!"

I scrambled to my feet. "Let's go, Jenny." I pulled her. She was glued to the cement block. Jackie took off without looking at any of us. Cindy scrambled out of the window after her. "Hurry!"

"I'm sopping wet; she'll know!" Jenny sobbed.

"Nobody cares!" I screeched. "It's dark. I promise, I promise she won't see." I shoved her up and we raced for the window. I dove out, tearing my shirt on the board and landing badly. "Come on, Jenny. Puhleeze!" She was frozen on the window ledge. "I can't. I'm stuck, I'm—"

"It's all right, okay, I'll climb back up and pull, I'm coming!"

A light flashed behind her. "Over there. Look, kids."

"No, Lucy! I've got it. Go! Run—please!"

"Jen—"

"Run!"

I felt like I had broken every single bone in both feet, but I ran. I caught up to Jackie and Cindy by Moore Avenue. "Go, go, go!" I yelled and glanced back once more. Oh God. . . .

We flew up Bayview, down Merton and up Cleveland. There it was, my Onlyhouse. I turned in and squeezed myself into a corner of the verandah. They whizzed past it. Nothing; no cops, no sirens, nothing.

After forever, I got up and let myself in. There it was again: boom, boom, boom, boom. I was clearly having a heart attack. I made a sign of the cross, told God I was sorry and waited to die. But I didn't. I crept over to the dirty laundry and got undressed. The shirt, I'd have to come up with something about the shirt. I boom-boomed all the way to the pullout couch.

Mama was breathing ever so softly, in and out, in and out. Just like nothing happened. Tears streamed down my face. "What a mess, what a mess. Mama!" I screamed in my head. "Mama, I'm sorry! Mama, what did I do? What can we do? They got her, Mama. The police got Jenny."

Chapter Thirteen

*I*t was Saturday morning and the sun was shining. I knew it was a miracle, but I couldn't remember why.

Somehow I got to the bathroom. I was brushing my teeth when it all came back—the Ouija board, the Bayview Ghost—God, Jenny. The room started spinning. I had to hold onto the sink. The cops would come today.

Mama had breakfast ready. "Good morning." She stopped. "Lucija, you don't look so good."

"I, uh, didn't sleep much." She felt my forehead. "I guess I'm worried about my project on ancient Rome." She smiled. "It's, uh, worth forty percent, you know." I had to think, think, think. We weren't going to the market. Taylor, Laidlaw and Abromovitz had a reception at their office on Friday. There would be extra cleaning. Good, we wouldn't be home when the cops came.

"Lucija, your shoes got so muddy," said Mama.

"Oh, well . . . uh . . ."

"While we were gardening," she said. "It's okay; I washed them."

"Yeah, gardening. And my shirt got a bit torn on the rose bush, too." God, lying was so easy.

She looked at me. "Maybe you should stay home

today. I know it's not much fun to be stuck inside cleaning on—"

"No! Really, no. I mean, I'm in a real cleaning mood, and there's so much to do today. Can we go now?"

Mama x-rayed me. "Eat your toast."

Taylor, Laidlaw and everybody were on the nine-teenth floor of the Toronto Dominion Building. As soon as Mama unlocked the reception doors, I headed straight for the boardroom. I emptied ashtrays and collected pencils. "Keep busy. Keep busy."

Mama vacuumed and I polished. She emptied garbage cans and I rinsed coffee cups. She scrubbed toilets and I washed sinks. Why, why, did I sneak out? I knew better. Why did I do it? I didn't want to do it. I almost didn't do it. But I did it. Why did I do it?

"Almost finished," called Mama.

Oh God. Back home.

There was a huge policeman in the subway. I thought he was going to get off at College, but instead he looked straight at me and started to come our way! Sweat oozed out of every single pore in my body, blood crashed around my head. I couldn't take it any-more. I looked right at him. "Okay, yes, I was there," I said. He walked right by us into the next subway car.

"Where, Lucija?" Mama turned to me.

"Oh, nowhere, Mama, nowhere really." For the next six subway stops, I smiled stupidly at the Chinese family crammed into the bench across from us. They didn't smile back.

Absolutely nobody phoned me except for Emily. She wanted me to come over and play Scrabble. I said I was busy.

"Okay. Fine, Lucy. I can take a hint. I'm not that stupid!"

"No, it's not—"

"Forget it. You can have your precious Tomcats. I hope you have a ball laughing at geeky Emily. I don't care. You don't have to *pretend* to like me anymore. You don't have to talk to me anymore."

"Emily, if you'd just—"

"In fact, I wouldn't talk to *you* if you were the last person on the planet."

Click.

Somehow Saturday turned into Sunday.

There was no way I was going to church. Uh-uh. St. Anselm's where we went now was one of those modern-type churches. You can barely make out that it's the Virgin Mary in the stained glass windows. Right behind the altar, there's this huge three-story beam of light all spray painted gold. Stuck on the beam is a two-story wooden cross, and stuck on the cross is a gigantic Jesus. Jesus is all spray painted gold, too. Well, because He's so high up there, He can see you no matter where you sit. If you were having a bad week, He'd look all hurt and disappointed. I wasn't going until I got to confession first.

Confession, God. God will forgive Catholics pretty well anything if they just confess. But I don't know—lying, sneaking out and cops—I had to figure out how to explain it so it wouldn't sound so awful. All of a sudden I missed the old neighborhood. It came in big waves of missing. I missed Shernee and Moshe, St. Therese's and the Sisters. All of a sudden I hated the Onlyhouse.

I told Mama I had a headache, a stomachache and my feet hurt. She went to church without me. I paced around all day waiting for the cops to come. I guess they don't arrest people on Sundays.

Emily really had given up on me. She wasn't waiting in front of my house on Monday morning. She wouldn't even look at me at school. That hurt; it hurt bad. I guess I was surprised she'd do it. I guess I was surprised it hurt. The rest of us acted like we didn't know each other. Jackie, Cindy and me, that is. Jenny wasn't there.

Just before recess, Jackie passed around a note:

Until we know what's what, we can't be seen together. Don't go to the clubhouse.

The note made it worse. I got an A+ on my "Life in Rome" project and burst into tears in the girls' washroom. I left my project at school.

Jenny didn't turn up on Tuesday or Wednesday either. What had they done with her? I kept trying to do normal grade six stuff, but Mama was worried. I could tell because she hovered. She was like a helicopter. Every so often she would stop hovering, swoop down and sit beside me. When nothing much happened she'd smile, get up and start hovering again.

Finally, on Wednesday night, during one of her swoops, she held position. "Lucija," she grimaced. She knew. God, she knew. "There comes a time when a young girl, well, when . . . a young girl becomes a woman. Well, not a woman, I guess. You're only eleven, but a young girl becomes, well, an older girl. It happens to everyone. Well, not to young boys, I guess. Anyway, these young older girls have bodies . . . that experience . . . certain . . ."

"Mama, relax!" I laughed. "My body is not having any experiences."

"Oh." She looked confused. "All right, if you're not you're not. But let me know when it happens. I've been practicing this since you were born."

"I will, Mama." I got up and gave her a killer hug. Then she really looked confused.

By Thursday I was almost getting used to walking to school by myself. I shuffled into class, sat down and stared at the clock. At three minutes to nine, Jenny walked in! Somebody gasped. She looked smaller as she walked by my desk. I kept staring at the back of her head, concentrating on every dirty blonde strand of hair. It was so good to see her alive and everything.

Jenny stayed in during recess, went straight home for lunch and stayed in for afternoon recess, too. I thought my brains were going to burst. When the bell rang at 3:45, she sprang to her feet and marched out. I didn't see the note until she was gone. My whole body was pounding. I tucked the note into my ancient Rome project and ran home.

I went straight to the kitchen and the uncrumpled paper. I read it and then read it again. I read it nine times and hugged the fridge. Jenny didn't talk!

Dear Lucy,

It's okay. I've written everyone. <u>I didn't tell who else was with me</u>. I'm grounded for the rest of the school year, including recess. It was real scary going home with the cops. My own fault. I'll tell you all about it as soon as I can. Thanks for trying to help.
Sincerely, your friend,

Me

She didn't talk! God! I was so stupendously proud of her—relieved, sure—but mainly stupendously proud. I couldn't wait for Mama to get home. I don't know why. I could hardly tell her that Jenny didn't talk. The door rattled open.

"Mama, guess what?"

"Well, hello to you, too," she laughed. "What, what is it?"

"Yes, what is it? It is great." I babbled. "It's great I got an A+ on my 'Life in Rome' story! It counts a whole lot for the school year."

"That's *perrrr*fect, Lucija. I'm very proud of you."

My face burned. "Mama—" I turned away.

"Yes, Lucija, yes!"

Was she angry?

"You are strong and smart and good. You think I don't know . . ." Her voice was shaky. "I know things. I see how . . . I know how different . . . me . . . us . . . all the girls here are . . . I'm sorry."

Somewhere in me was a little pointy hurt. I couldn't find it because it moved around at lightning speed: head, heart, stomach, knees, head . . .

I grabbed hold of her. "No, Mama! You're better than perfect. You got us the Onlyhouse, the Christmas tree. I'm the one who's proud, I promise. I promise!" Mama hugged back. Her arms found the hurt, froze it and melted it away.

I practically skipped to school on Friday. It hardly mattered that Emily wasn't with me. I caught up to Jackie in the hallway. "Hi ya!" I beamed.

"Shhh. Not now. Just to be double sure." She looked around. "Let's meet at the swing set in the school yard, 4:30."

"You got it." I bounced over to my desk. We all kept our distance over recess, but Cindy and I kept grinning and winking at each other across the yard. As soon as school ended, I sped home. I washed and chopped the vegetables for dinner. Just before leaving, I broke open the seal and carefully applied my Sand-pebble Beige lipstick by Bonnie Bell.

104

Purple rain clouds hung over the playground. Jackie was there by herself, making figure eights on the swing. "Hi!" I called. "Where's Cindy?"

"Hi, yourself," she grinned. "I didn't tell her to come. I thought it should be just us. Hey!" She jumped off the swing. "Can you believe it? I thought I was cooked."

"Yeah," I snorted. "I kept throwing up and waiting for the cops."

"Ha!" she threw back her head and howled. "Too much, eh? Who'd have thought that little fart-face could keep her stupid mouth shut?"

My stomach twisted. I stared at her. "Huh?" I said.

"Course the reject knew I'd destroy her, and I'm still going to for getting caught in the first place."

This was going all wrong. "Jackie, she's getting punished because of us. She's grounded. The rest of her school year is ruined because of us."

"So? It serves the little twit right," she shrugged. "Why didn't she take off? I'll tell you why, she choked. I've known her a lot longer than you have and believe me, Jenny Clarke always chokes, always, always, always."

"She didn't choke! She didn't jump because she was so—" I stopped. "Because she hurt herself."

"What's with you?" she asked. "So she choked and she's uncoordinated. Am I supposed to congratulate her because she's spastic? I learned a long time ago to look after number one first!" She thumped her chest.

"Jackie! She didn't talk!" I yelled. "We'd all be in prison if it weren't for her. It took guts not to talk."

"Get real." Her eyes shot like bullets. "She knew I'd kill her if she opened her fat mouth. The Tomcats are well rid of her. Good riddance."

"Jackie . . . that's not—"

"We'll get someone else!" she spat. "Susan Ambrose

105

is dying to get in; so is Lisa Kirkland. Who gives a damn?"

A storm crackled in my head. Thunder rumbled and I felt a drop. "I do," I whispered. "You can get her to take my place. I quit." I said it, I know I said it. Those words came out of my mouth. I couldn't believe it. Neither could Jackie.

"What?" she said.

"I want out, Jackie."

"Don't be a jerk!" She was glaring and smiling at the same time. "Look, you want Jenny in, she's in. It was just a joke. Can't you take a joke?"

"No." Raindrops exploded in the sand around us. She got up to touch me. I moved away.

"Are you sick?" she asked.

"I guess I am." I said. "I'm sick of doing sick things. You're mean, Jackie. You're just so . . . *mean.*"

"It's that immigrant mother of yours," she spat. "She's making you do this."

"You leave my mama out of this!" I stared at my shoes.

"We're blood brothers, Lucy." Her voice cracked. "You can't leave me, too. You promised at the cemetery. You promised, remember?"

"I know." It was wrong, bad to break a promise. "I'm sorry about that. I'm sorry about this."

"You're just like everyone else!"

"No." I said. "You were right before, a long time ago. I am different. I'm different from you. I gotta go."

"Wait!" She screamed. "I can fix things."

I kept walking.

"I'll give you five seconds. We'll pretend it never happened. Best friends have fights all the time. Okay? Five . . . four . . . three . . . two . . . one. . . . Come back here. . . . Lucy, please!"

God, I started to turn.

"You're not a Somebody, Lucy." She was laughing! "You're a *Nobody*. Nothing. Zero. Go back to where you came from. Immigrant pig."

It'll be okay. It'll be okay. I kept walking.

"Go home and light some candles you filthy Catholic. You never belonged and you never will. I'll make them all hate you!"

I got to Cleveland Street. She was still screaming, but I could barely hear her. I was so scared. Wait a minute. No, I wasn't. I wasn't scared. I was angry! Hey! I shot off blinding retorts and scathing replies. I was cruel. I was wounding. I was completely alone, talking to myself on Cleveland Street.

"Alone? That's okay. I can be alone. So who needs friends?" I muttered, crossing Millwood. "Just a few weeks till school's over. Yeah. Then next year, it's Hodgson Senior Public School. Yeah. It'll be full of new kids. I'll make millions of friends and they'll all really like me. Yeah. What's not to like?"

By the time I got to the Onlyhouse, the rain had stopped. The street was shiny and still.

No. It wasn't okay. I couldn't go that long without friends. I lumbered up the stairs. I was sopping wet, but instead of getting changed I sat in front of the phone. I stared and stared at it. I was almost dry by the time I picked it up. I took a huge breath and dialed. I swallowed hard and waited.

"Hello."

"Hi," I said. "How are you, Emily?"

"Lucy?"

"Yeah. Please don't hang up, Emily. I feel like I'm the last person on the planet, and I haven't got anyone to talk to."

Epilogue

*T*he phone rang again last night. I let it ring six times, then answered it. A dial tone was all I heard. Whoever it was had hung up again. It had happened every few days all summer long, the ringing, the hanging up.

I knew it was Jackie.

Aside from the ringing, it was the most amazing, best, perfect summer of my life. It was a summer, a summer like I didn't even deserve.

The McDonalds invited me to spend the first two weeks of July at their cottage with them, Emily and the black flies. God, do black flies love Croatians. Mrs. McDonald said she'd never seen anything like it. Emily and I would go for a walk in the woods, and she'd come back with three bites. Meanwhile my eyes were swollen shut and every visible and invisible piece of my skin was covered with bruised red bumps. I thought I was dying. We had to make a special trip to the village store to get some industrial strength bug spray. It was better after that except nobody could stand sitting close to me.

The cottage was in the woods by a lake. It was Mr. McDonald's great great grandfather's place and he built it with a bunch of logs. Inside, the ceilings were wood, the walls were wood, the floors were wood and, of course, the furniture was wood. "Knotty pine," said Mrs. McDonald. It was nice and everything but since we were in the middle of a forest to begin with, it was a bit much with all those trees inside and outside. It got so that I missed the smell of steaming asphalt after a good hot rain.

Oh, and another thing—they had an outhouse! That's a bathroom way outside with no plumbing! The McDonalds can afford a big motorboat, a dock, a whole lot of land and a cottage, but they can't afford an indoor toilet? I will never understand these people.

Anyway, Emily and I spent all day every day in the water—electric magic! We pretended to be those wicked mermaids, I forget their names, the ones who lured sailors to their deaths with their incredible beauty and hypnotic singing. Most of Emily's cottage neighbors played along except for the crash and death part.

At night, if we weren't going to somebody's barbecue or hosting our own, we worked on our second mystery novel, *The Frozen Ghost*. We named the chief inspector Carole Lewis. This one is going to get published for sure. We're going to do exactly twelve more in this series. Each one is going to have something to do with temperature in the title, like *The Melting Corpses* and *The Tepid Terrorist*. Emily is a walking thesaurus.

Sometimes we'd all stay up really late and sit out on the dock. Mr. McDonald would go on and on about star formations and the aurora borealis. I didn't always get what he was talking about, but I could listen to him forever.

When we got home, the McDonalds spent half an hour thanking Mama for letting *me* come and stay with *them*. As soon as they left, Mama burst into tears.

Mama took a whole week's holiday at the end of July. Her first ever. I mean, no cafeteria, no part-time catering, no office cleaning, nothing. We went to Centre Island on the ferry for three days straight. We couldn't afford the rides and stuff, but we took a fabulous picnic to Hanna's Point every day. We left on the very last ferry each night.

One day we walked from our house all the way down to Yonge and Queen and went to Simpson's. We had lunch at the Arcadian Court. Our waiter was gone and so was the man playing the piano, but we had an absolutely *perrrr*fect hamburger.

One Friday, both Emily and Jenny Clarke slept over. Well, actually we didn't sleep. We stayed up all night and then went to the Jewish market at 6:30 a.m. on Saturday. Were they impressed! They still can't figure out how we got the Christmas tree all the way home from Goldman's. We've all decided that having a bedroom in the dining room is perfect. Sometimes I believe it.

In August, Jenny and I signed up for volleyball and softball at the Parks and Rec at Davisville Park. We were brilliant. We decided we'd try out for basketball, volleyball, track *and* gymnastics at Hodgson. Jenny never hung around with Jackie anymore. Her parents wouldn't let her. She didn't tell them about . . . well, about that night, but they still wouldn't let her. Jenny said that was okay by her. Cindy had gone away to her cottage for the whole summer. She didn't call either of us to say good-bye.

I never talked about Jackie.

I never once said her name.

Today was the first day for basketball tryouts. Today was my first day at Hodgson Senior Public

School. I ran out of the house as soon as I saw Emily reach the tip of my sidewalk.

"Emily, your hair ribbons match your socks, for God sakes! This is *senior* public school."

I was wearing one of the hair bands that Gitta, our invisible German tenant, had given me. Gitta went to the old country for a month, and she came back with six wild multicolored hair bands for me! What could Mama do? I had to wear genuine souvenirs. I have *uninvisibled* Gitta.

"I know, I know," Emily moaned. "Explain that to my mother."

"Come on."

We were meeting Jenny at the corner of Cleveland and Davisville. Was that her?

"Wow!"

Jenny Clarke had gotten her hair cut off—I mean all cut off! It was like a boy's. We all had long hair, all of us, every one, all the time. Jenny's, well, now you couldn't even stick a barrette in it!

"You look *great!*" I hugged her.

"Really, absolutely, really," said Emily.

"She means it," I said. "Her dimple's showing."

Jenny fired up bright red. "Yeah, thanks, I kind of like it. It'll be great for basketball, eh, Lucy?"

"That's right. Let's go, guys."

As soon as we got to the corner right before the school yard, we heard the chanting.

"Fight. Fight. Fight. Fight. Fight."

The three of us ran up to the fence. There it was, a huge ring of kids, strange faces, angry faces. Was that Cindy's face in the ring? Yeah, it was Cindy! She saw us and sort of smiled. It was the same smile she had when she ran into the club with the lipstick. The ring shifted and we could see the middle. There was a real tough-looking girl with lots of makeup on, a grade eighter maybe. She was being pounded and destroyed by this—God, *Jackie!* I stared at her and stared back at Cindy. She waved this time. I was the only one who waved back.

"Let's *go,*" said Emily.

"Yeah," said Jenny. "There's a great spot between the portables."

"You know," I said as we walked away, "all summer long my phone's been ringing, and when I pick it up, they hang up."

"I hate that," said Emily.

"Yeah, it's creepy," said Jenny.

"Yeah, well . . . I think it's Jackie."

They nodded.

"In fact, I know it's Jackie."

They nodded.

"One day, well, one day I'm going to go right up to her and say 'I know it's you on the phone.' And then I'm going to point right at her and say, 'Jackie, people who are *Somebodies* don't just phone up other people and hang up. Only cowards do that.'"

They nodded.

"I'm going to do that."

They nodded.

"One day."